FAR OUT
CLASSIC STORIES

STONE ARCH BOOKS
a capstone imprint

INTRODUCING...

ALICE

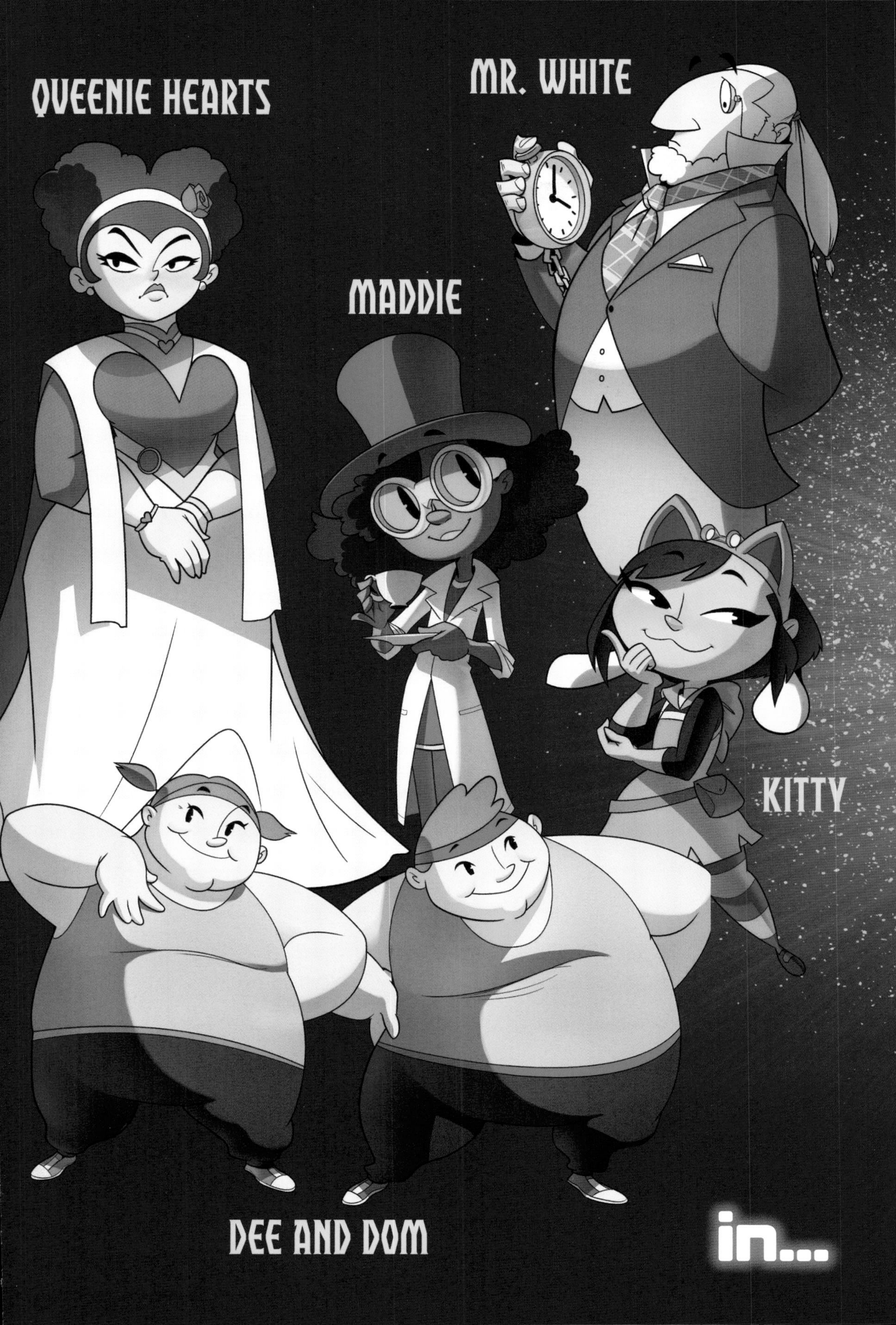
QUEENIE HEARTS
MR. WHITE
MADDIE
KITTY
DEE AND DOM
in...

Far Out Classic Stories is published by
Stone Arch Books,
an imprint of Capstone.
1710 Roe Crest Drive
North Mankato, Minnesota 56003
www.capstonepub.com

Library of Congress Cataloging-in-
Publication Data is available on the
Library of Congress website.
ISBN: 978-1-4965-8684-1 (hardcover)
ISBN: 978-1-4965-9192-0 (paperback)
ISBN: 978-1-4965-8685-8 (eBook PDF)

Summary: Alice is a super-serious
pre-teen secret agent, but her new
team at Wonderland is . . . odd.
Mr. White, the new boss, is always
running late. Maddie makes wacky spy
hats. And Alice's new partner, Kitty,
keeps disappearing. How can Alice stop
the evil Queenie Hearts's top-secret
plan amid all this madness?

Designed by Hilary Wacholz
Edited by Abby Huff
Lettered by Jaymes Reed

Printed and bound in the USA.
PA99

FAR OUT CLASSIC STORIES

ALICE, SECRET AGENT OF WONDERLAND

A GRAPHIC NOVEL

BY KATIE SCHENKEL

ILLUSTRATED BY FERN CANO

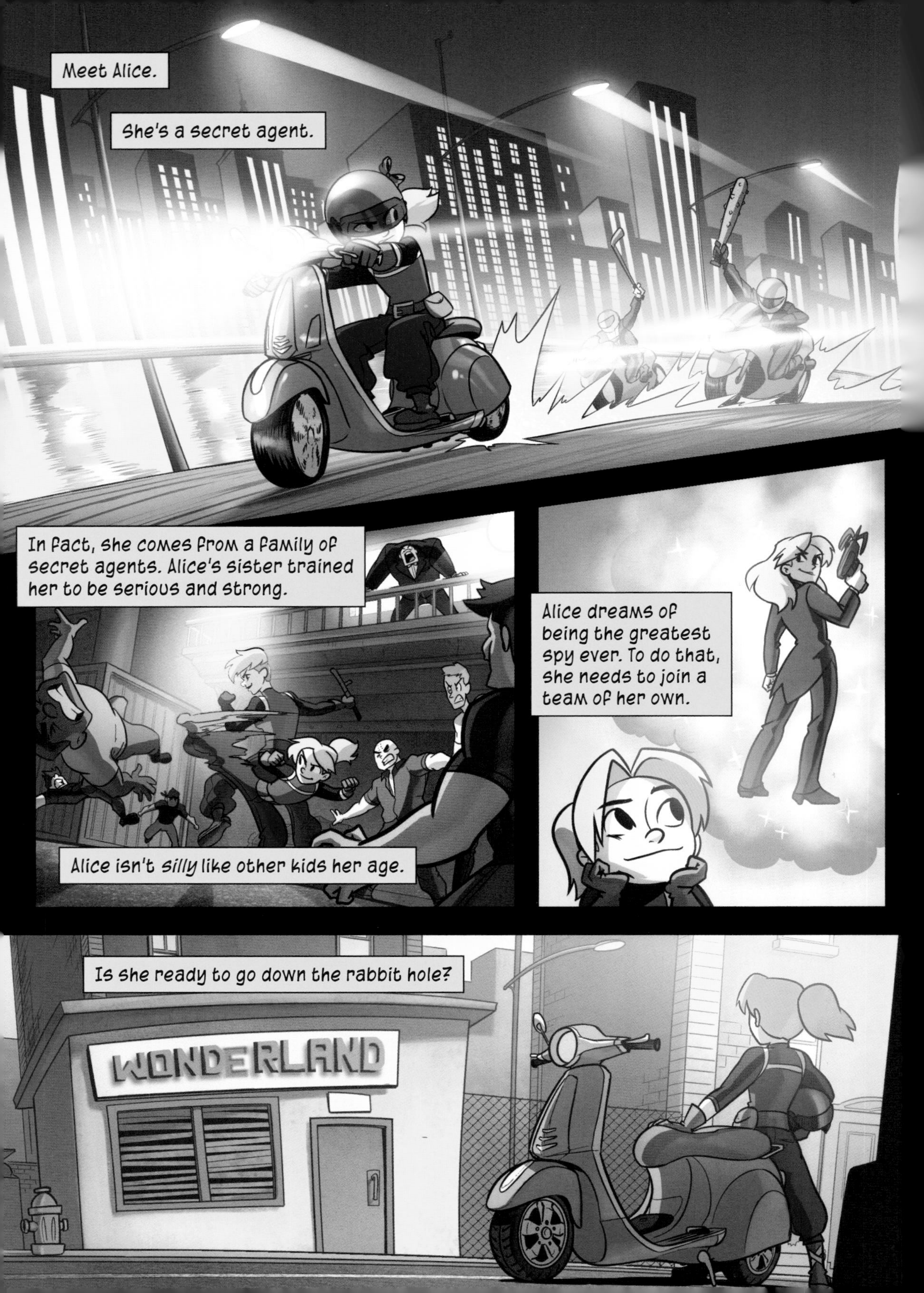
Meet Alice.
She's a secret agent.
In fact, she comes from a family of secret agents. Alice's sister trained her to be serious and strong.
Alice isn't *silly* like other kids her age.
Alice dreams of being the greatest spy ever. To do that, she needs to join a team of her own.
Is she ready to go down the rabbit hole?
WONDERLAND

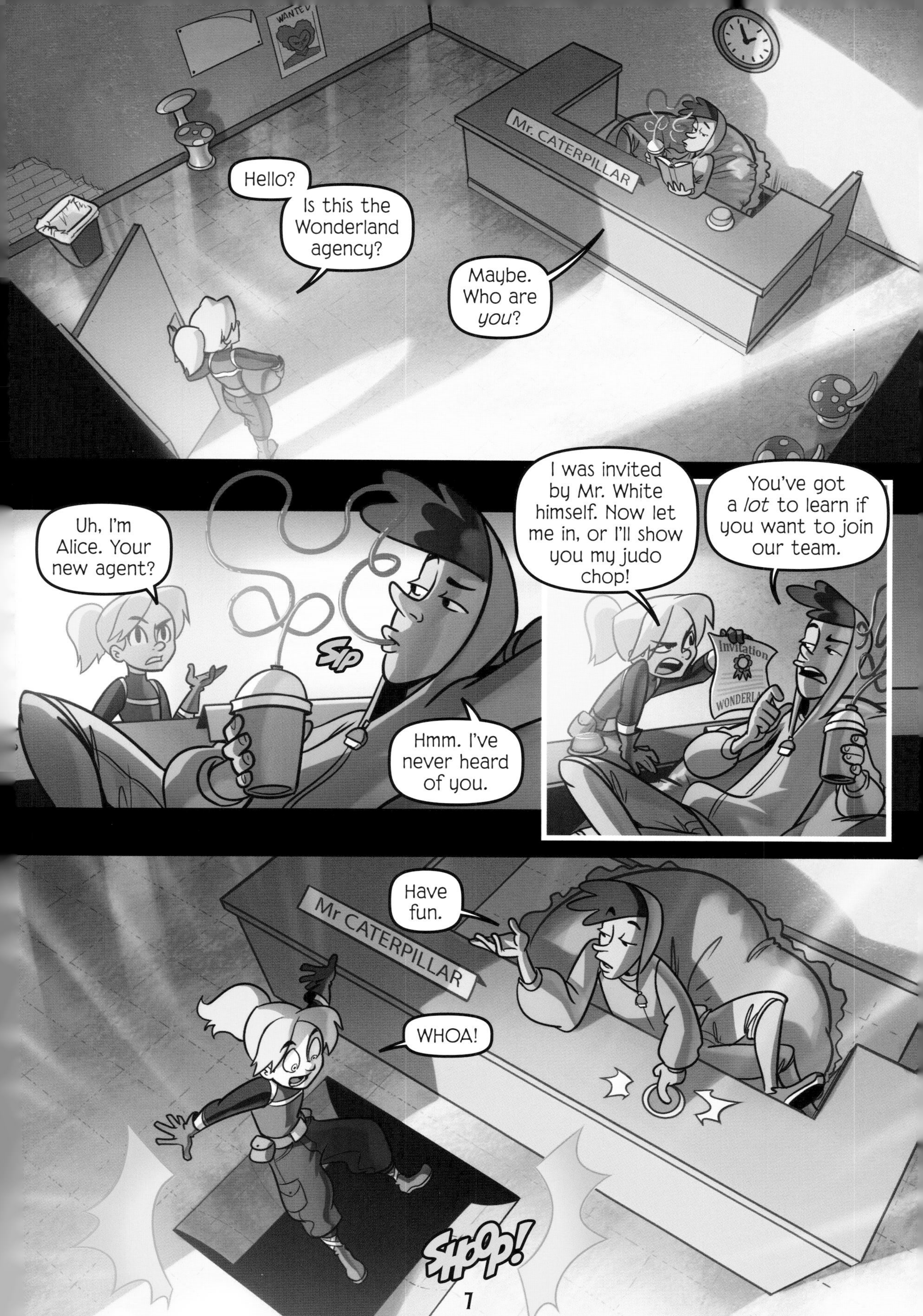
WANTED
Mr. CATERPILLAR
Hello?
Is this the Wonderland agency?
Maybe. Who are *you*?
Uh, I'm Alice. Your new agent?
SIP
Hmm. I've never heard of you.
I was invited by Mr. White himself. Now let me in, or I'll show you my judo chop!
Invitation
You've got a *lot* to learn if you want to join our team.
Mr CATERPILLAR
Have fun.
WHOA!
SHOOP!

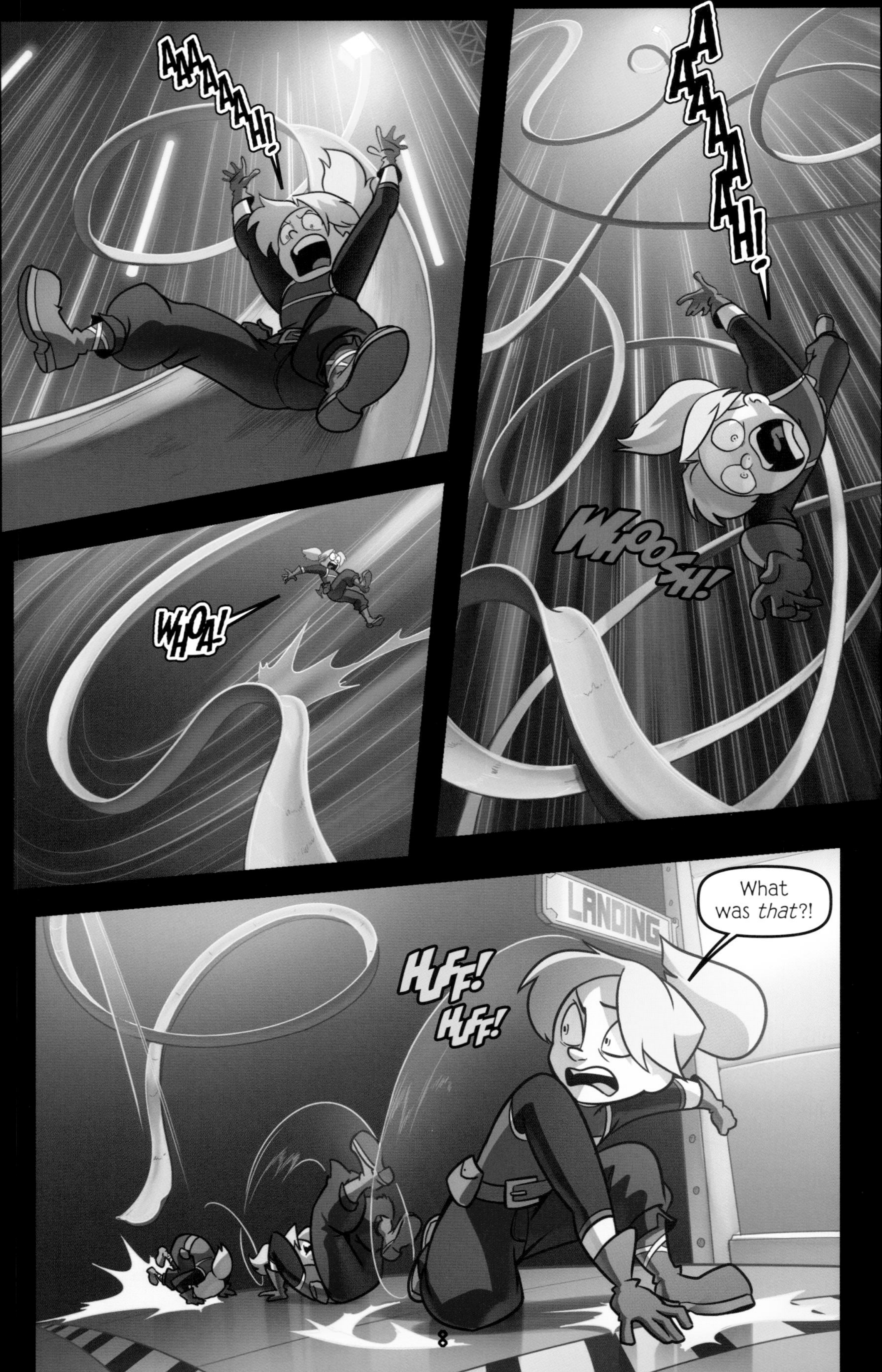
AAAAAAAH!
AAAAAAAAH!
WHOOSH!
WHOA!
LANDING
HUFF! HUFF!
What was *that*?!

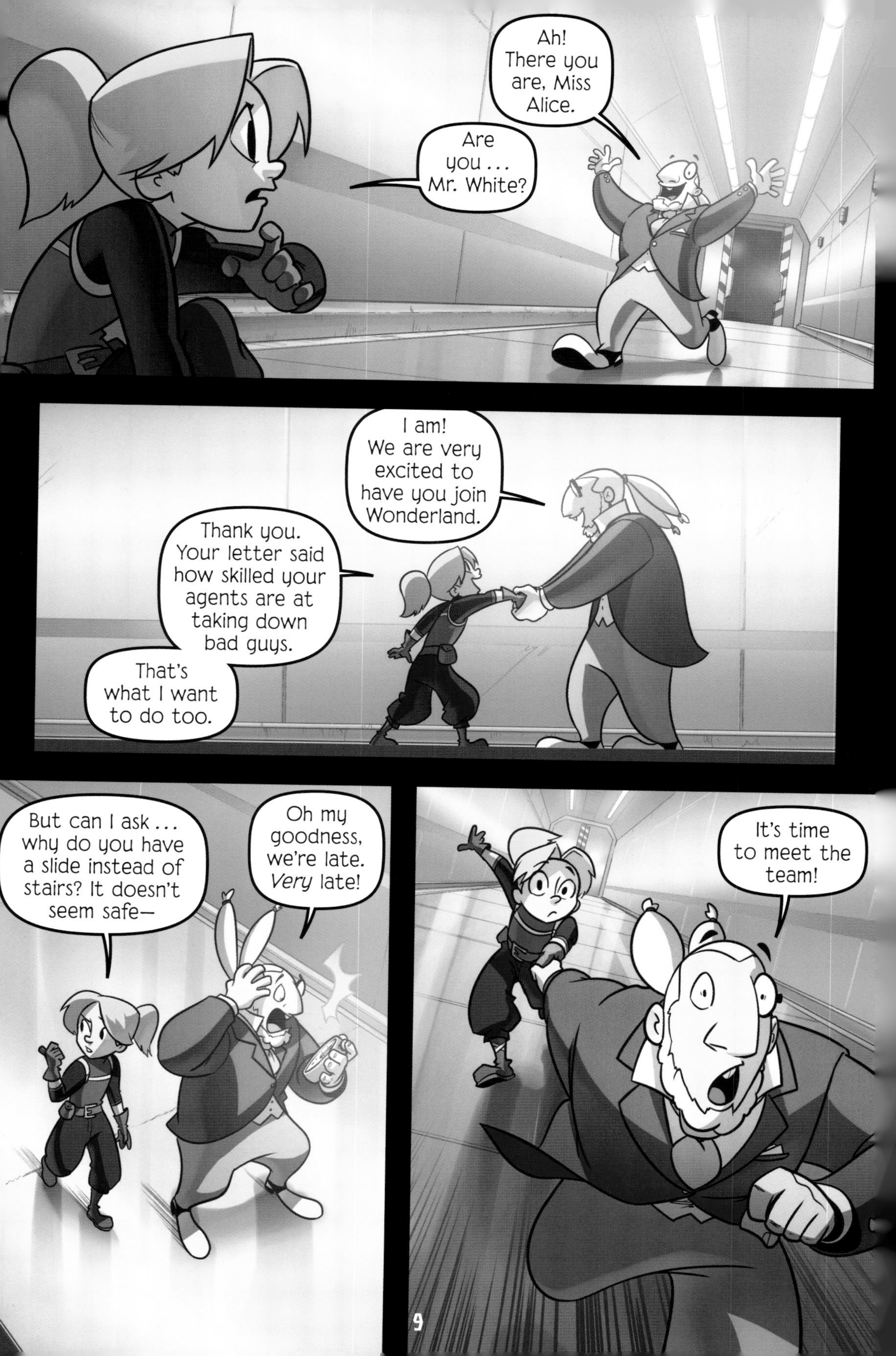
Ah! There you are, Miss Alice.
Are you . . . Mr. White?
I am! We are very excited to have you join Wonderland.
Thank you. Your letter said how skilled your agents are at taking down bad guys.
That's what I want to do too.
But can I ask . . . why do you have a slide instead of stairs? It doesn't seem safe—
Oh my goodness, we're late. *Very* late!
It's time to meet the team!

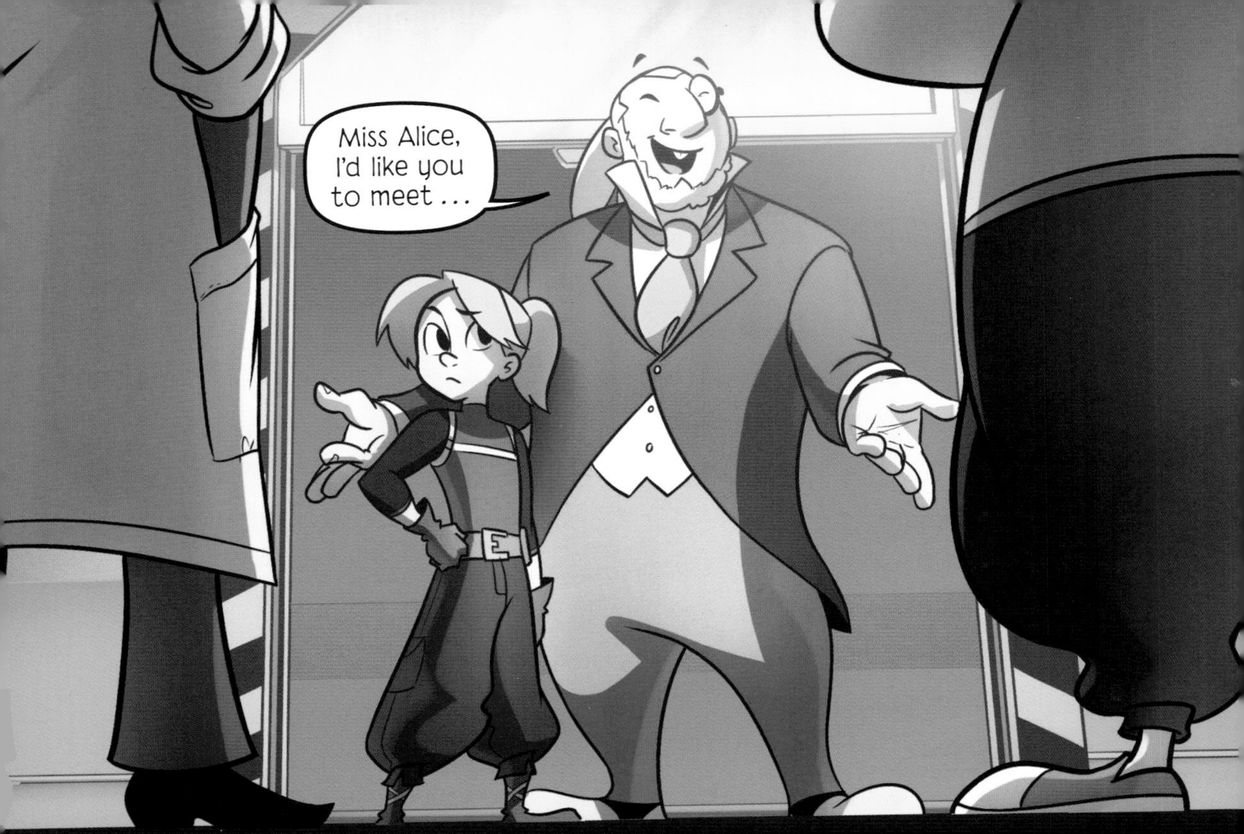
Miss Alice, I'd like you to meet . . .

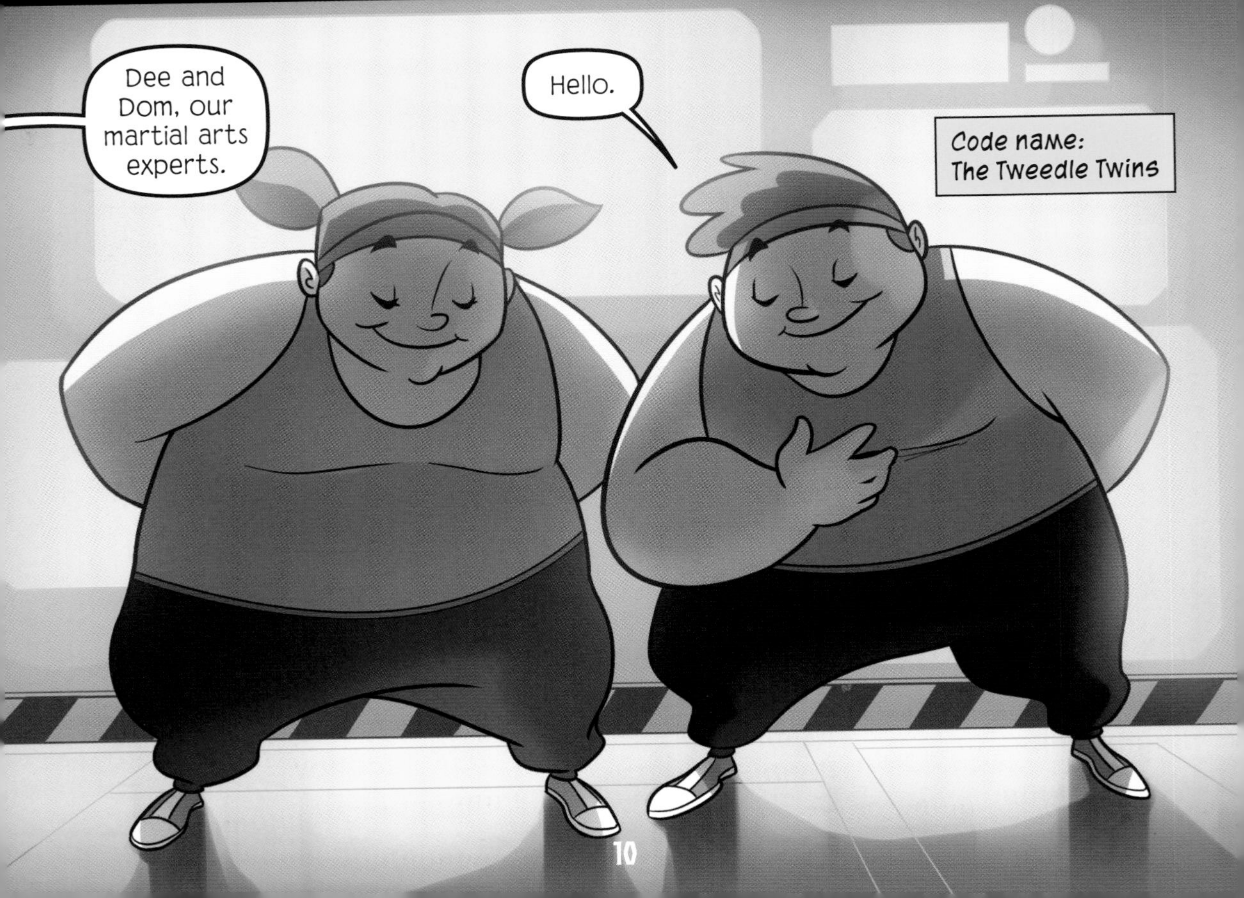
Dee and Dom, our martial arts experts.
Hello.
Code name: The Tweedle Twins

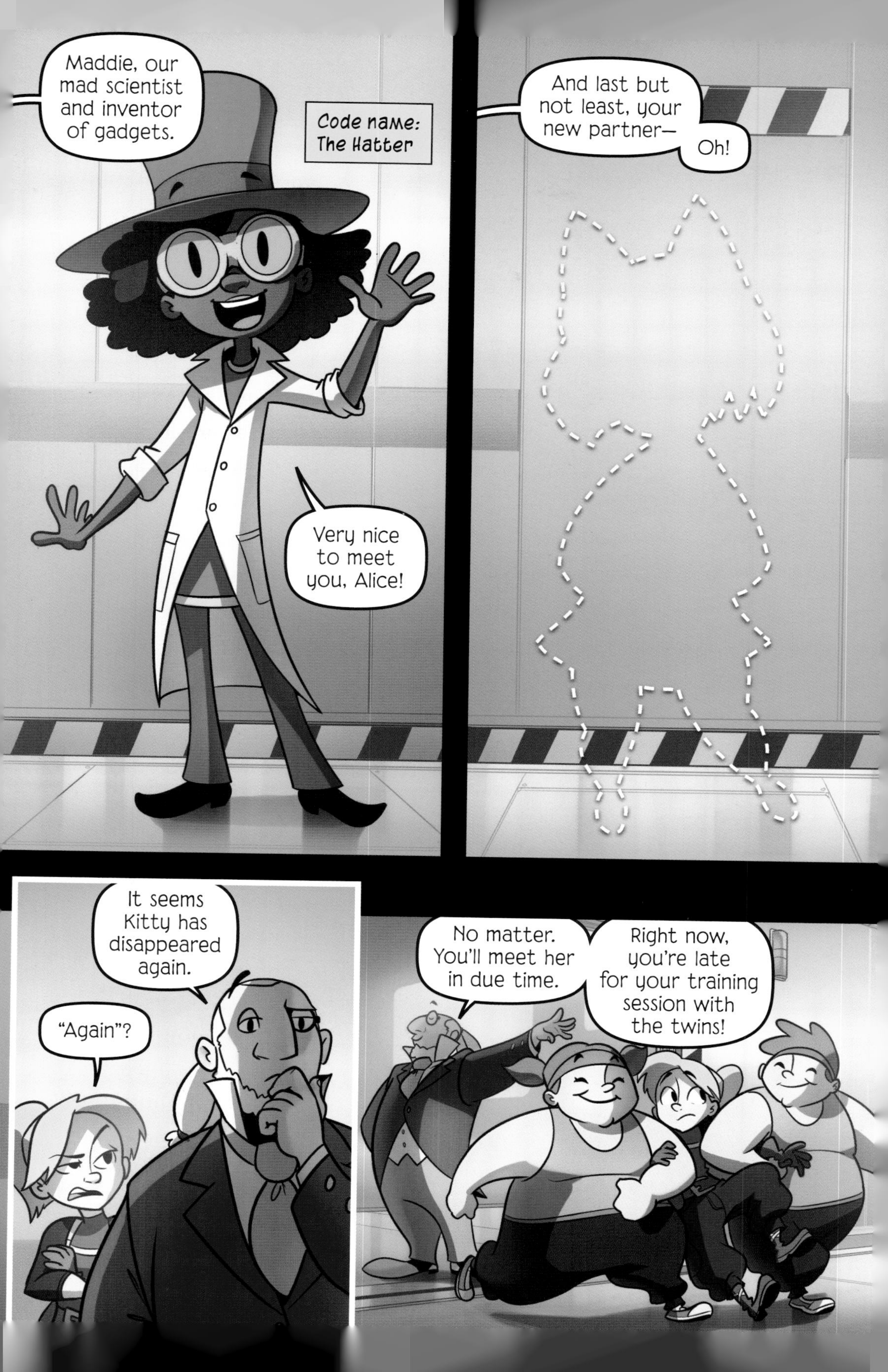

Maddie, our mad scientist and inventor of gadgets.
Code name: The Hatter
Very nice to meet you, Alice!
And last but not least, your new partner—
Oh!
It seems Kitty has disappeared again.
"Again"?
No matter. You'll meet her in due time.
Right now, you're late for your training session with the twins!

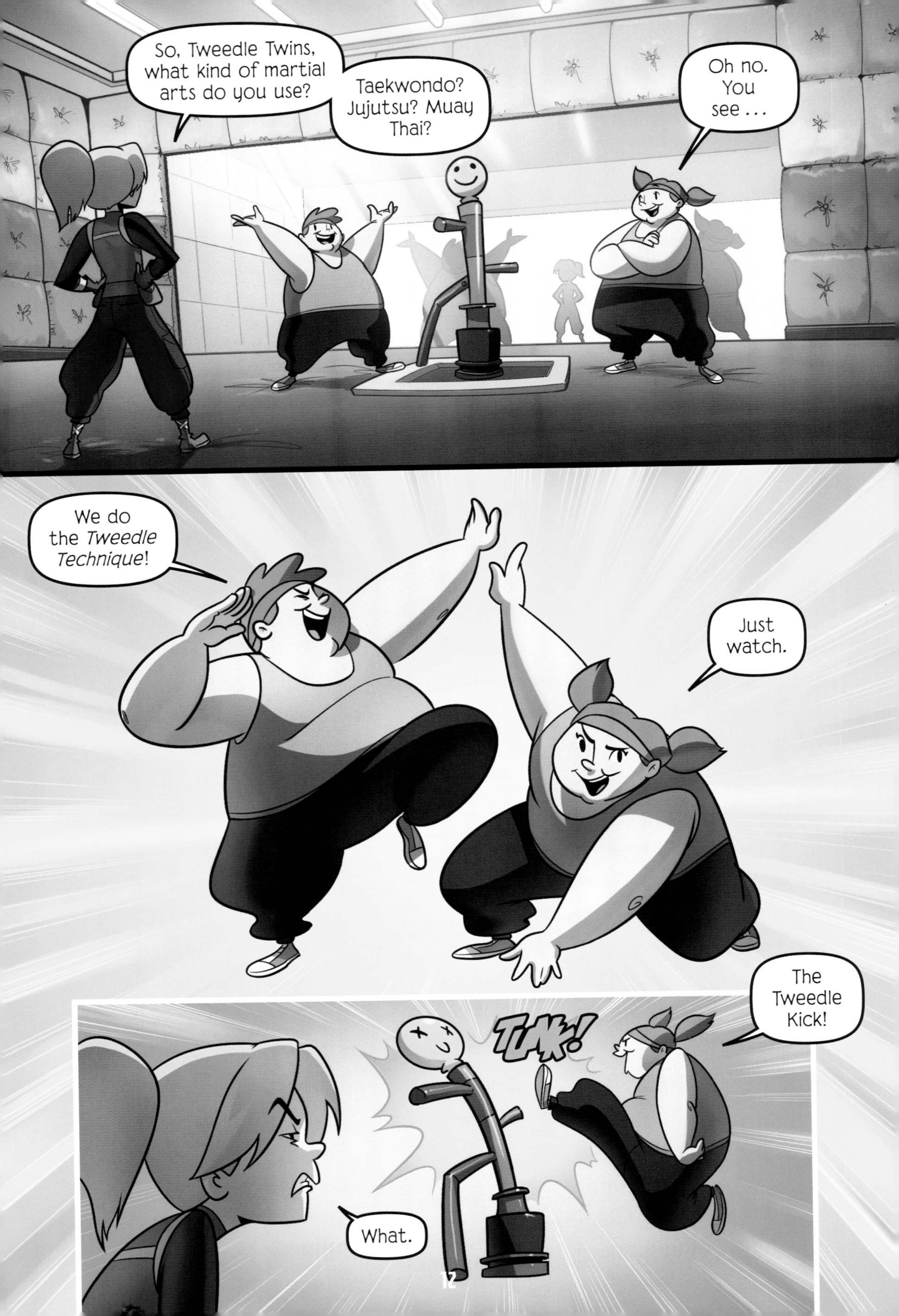

So, Tweedle Twins, what kind of martial arts do you use?
Taekwondo? Jujutsu? Muay Thai?
Oh no. You see . . .
We do the *Tweedle Technique*!
Just watch.
TUNK!
The Tweedle Kick!
What.

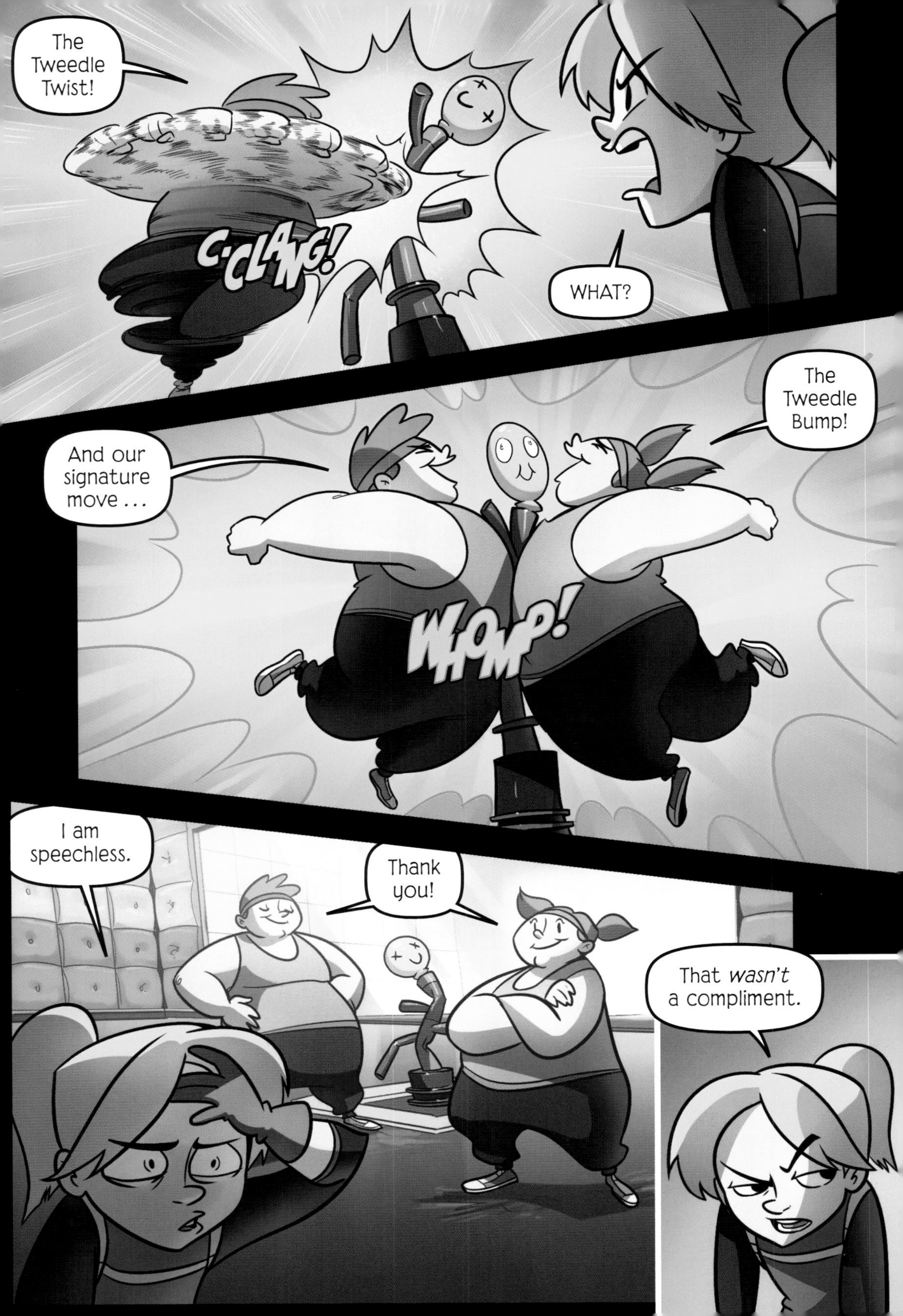
The Tweedle Twist!
C-CLANG!
WHAT?
And our signature move . . .
The Tweedle Bump!
WHOMP!
I am speechless.
Thank you!
That *wasn't* a compliment.

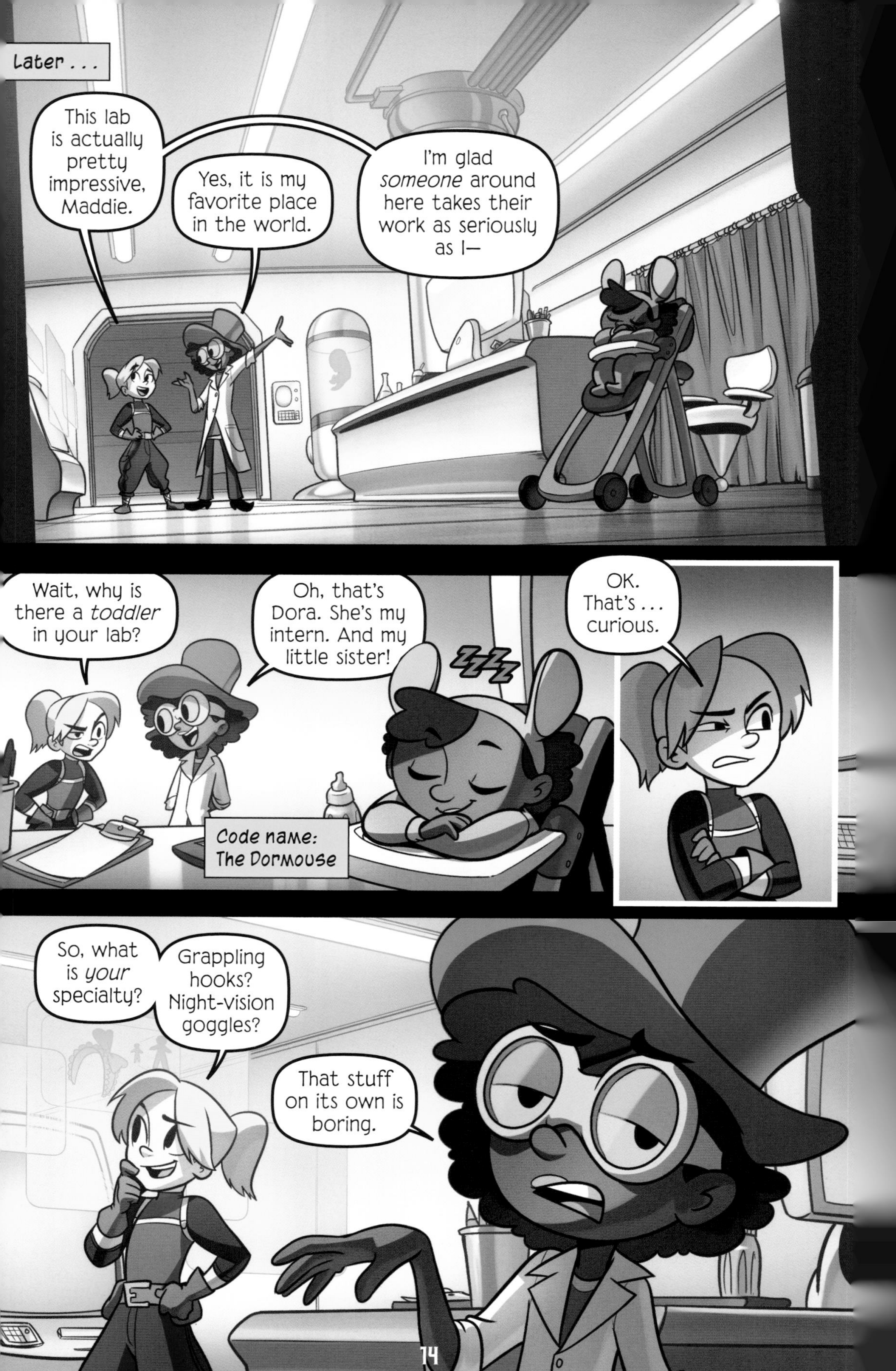
Later . . .
This lab is actually pretty impressive, Maddie.
Yes, it is my favorite place in the world.
I'm glad *someone* around here takes their work as seriously as I—
Wait, why is there a *toddler* in your lab?
Oh, that's Dora. She's my intern. And my little sister!
ZZZ
Code name: The Dormouse
OK. That's . . . curious.
So, what is *your* specialty?
Grappling hooks? Night-vision goggles?
That stuff on its own is boring.

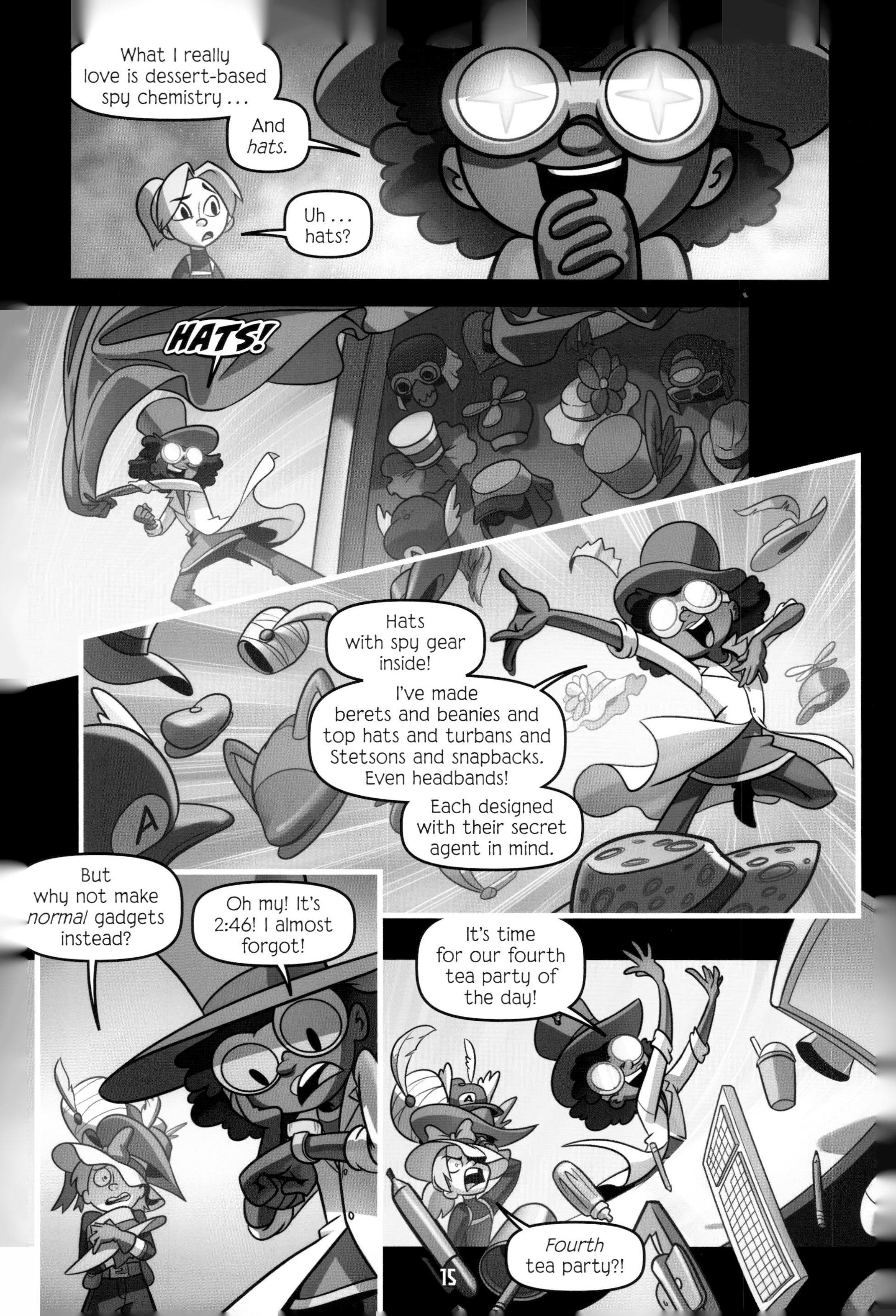
What I really love is dessert-based spy chemistry . . .
And *hats.*
Uh . . . hats?
HATS!
Hats with spy gear inside!
I've made berets and beanies and top hats and turbans and Stetsons and snapbacks. Even headbands!
Each designed with their secret agent in mind.
But why not make *normal* gadgets instead?
Oh my! It's 2:46! I almost forgot!
It's time for our fourth tea party of the day!
Fourth tea party?!

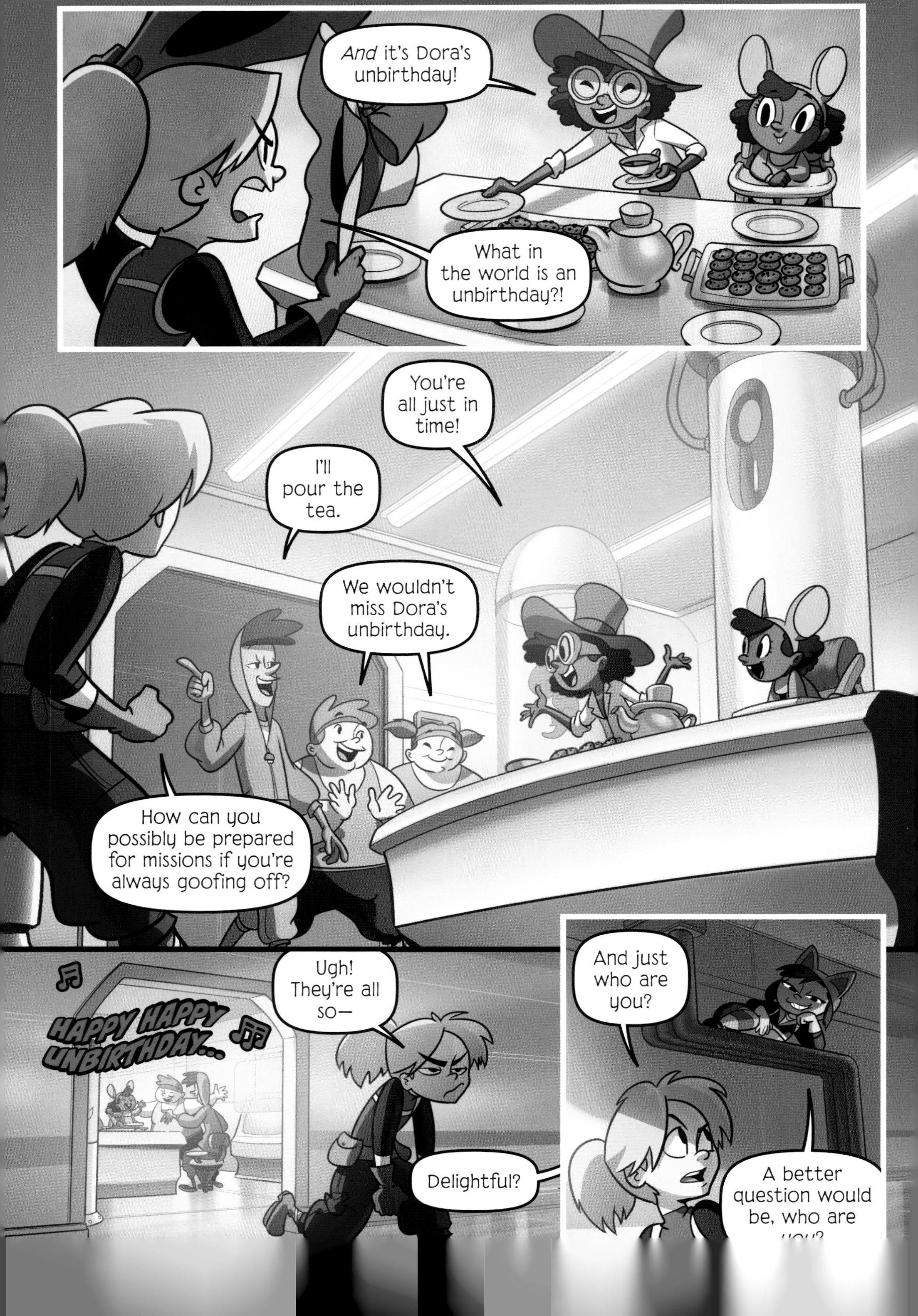

And it's Dora's unbirthday!
What in the world is an unbirthday?!
You're all just in time!
I'll pour the tea.
We wouldn't miss Dora's unbirthday.
How can you possibly be prepared for missions if you're always goofing off?
HAPPY HAPPY UNBIRTHDAY...
Ugh! They're all so—
Delightful?
And just who are you?
A better question would be, who are

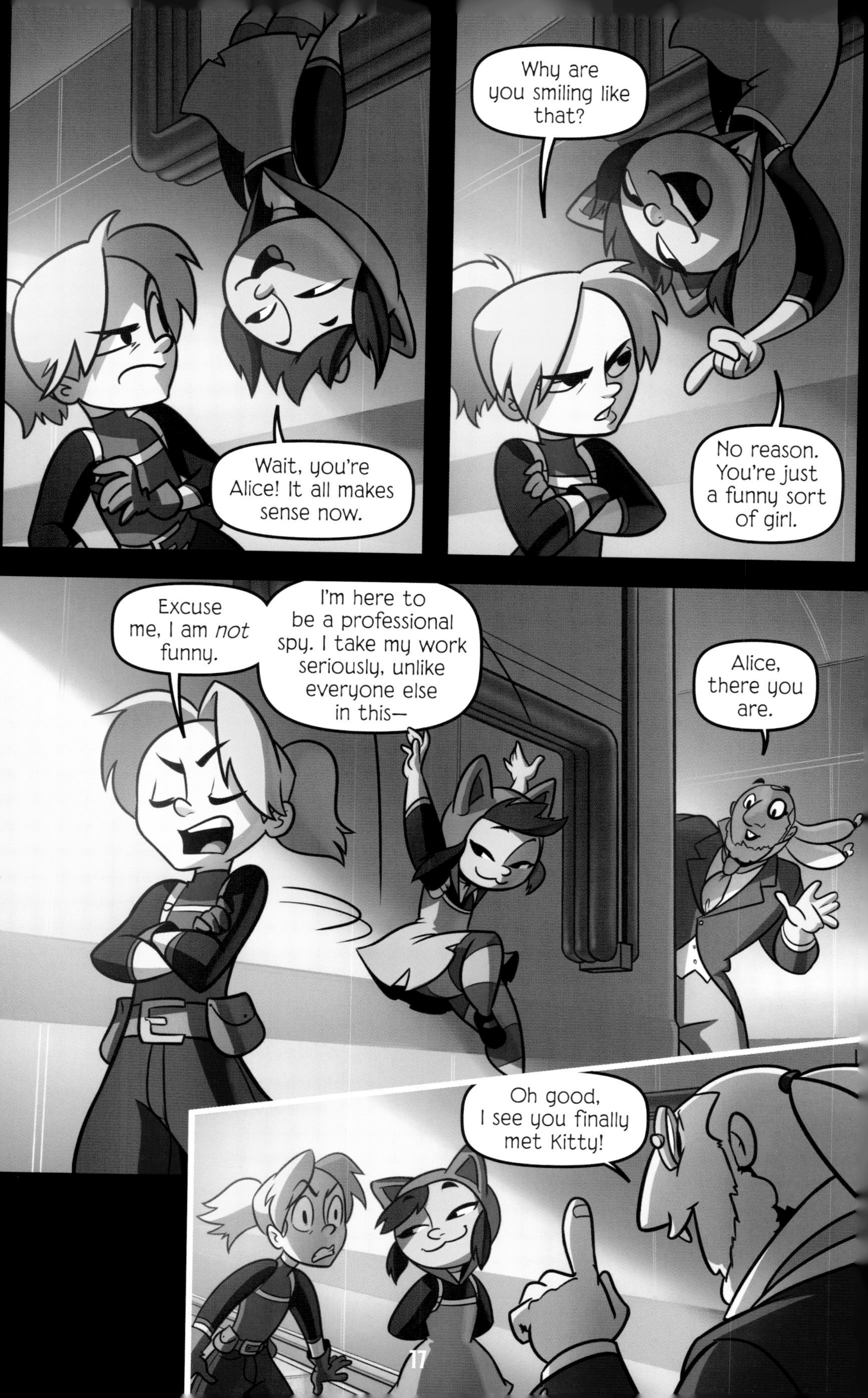
Wait, you're Alice! It all makes sense now.
Why are you smiling like that?
No reason. You're just a funny sort of girl.
Excuse me, I am *not* funny.
I'm here to be a professional spy. I take my work seriously, unlike everyone else in this—
Alice, there you are.
Oh good, I see you finally met Kitty!

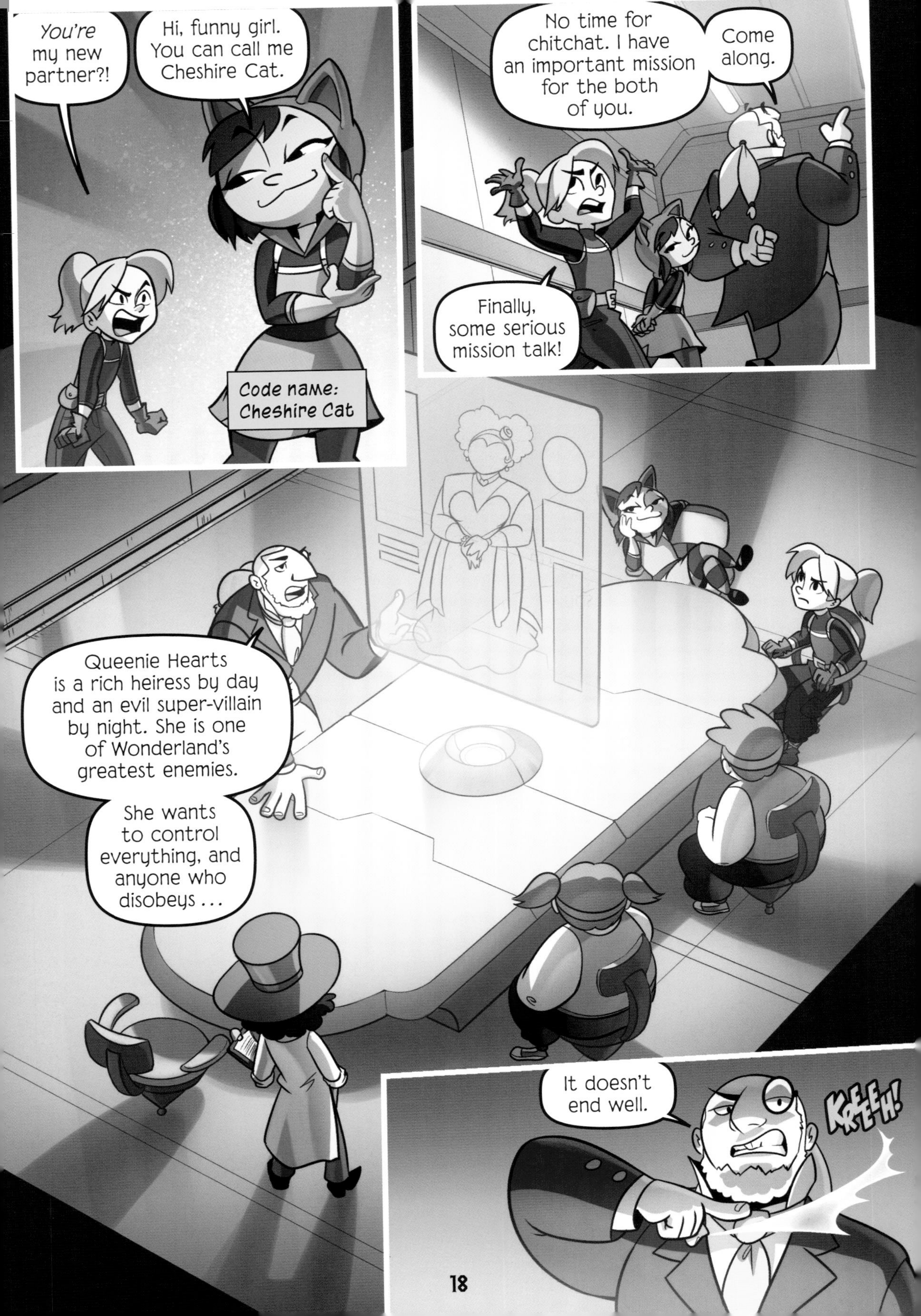

You're my new partner?!
Hi, funny girl. You can call me Cheshire Cat.
Code name: Cheshire Cat
No time for chitchat. I have an important mission for the both of you.
Come along.
Finally, some serious mission talk!
Queenie Hearts is a rich heiress by day and an evil super-villain by night. She is one of Wonderland's greatest enemies.
She wants to control everything, and anyone who disobeys . . .
It doesn't end well.
KREEEH!

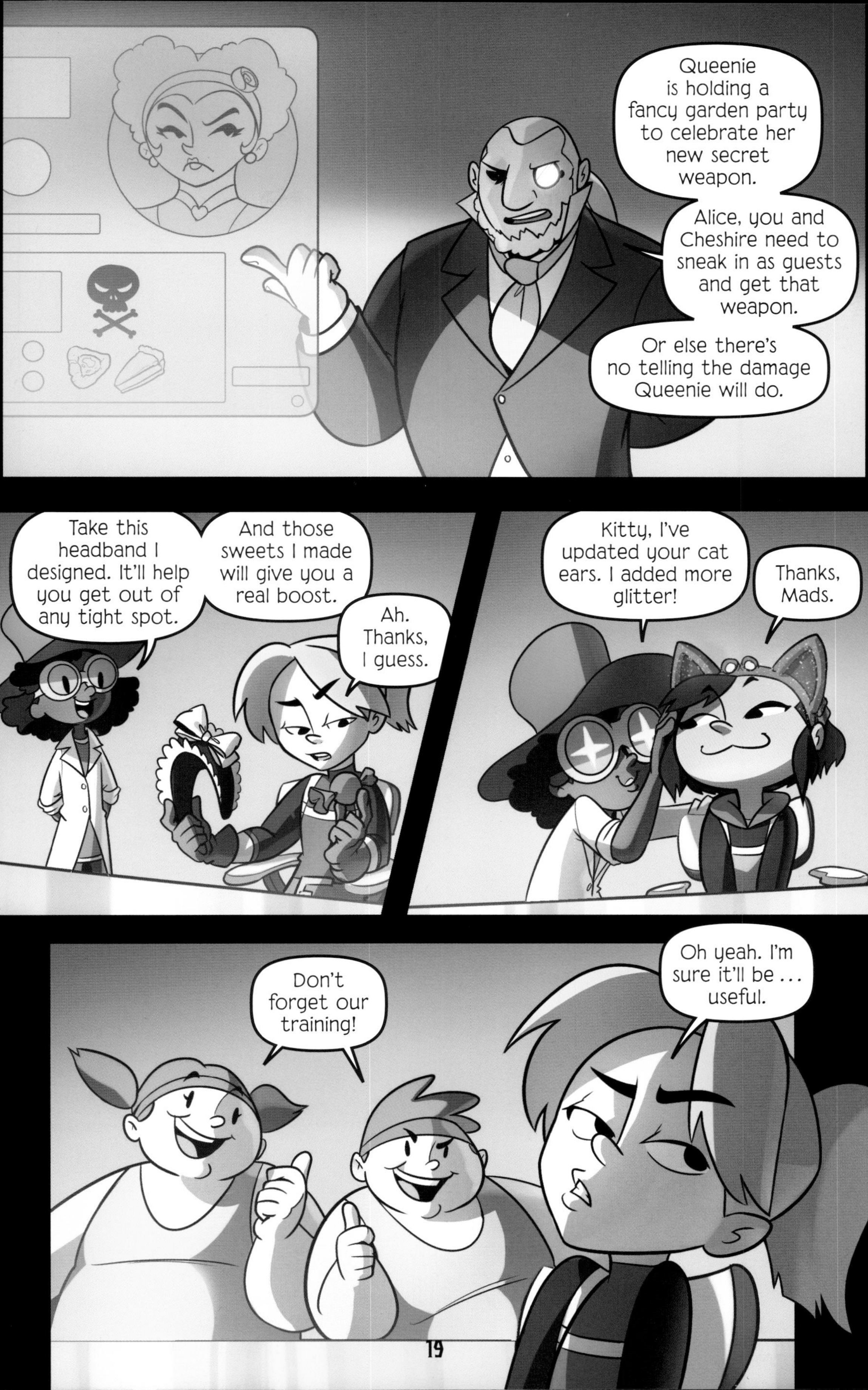
Queenie is holding a fancy garden party to celebrate her new secret weapon.
Alice, you and Cheshire need to sneak in as guests and get that weapon.
Or else there's no telling the damage Queenie will do.
Take this headband I designed. It'll help you get out of any tight spot.
And those sweets I made will give you a real boost.
Ah. Thanks, I guess.
Kitty, I've updated your cat ears. I added more glitter!
Thanks, Mads.
Don't forget our training!
Oh yeah. I'm sure it'll be . . . useful.

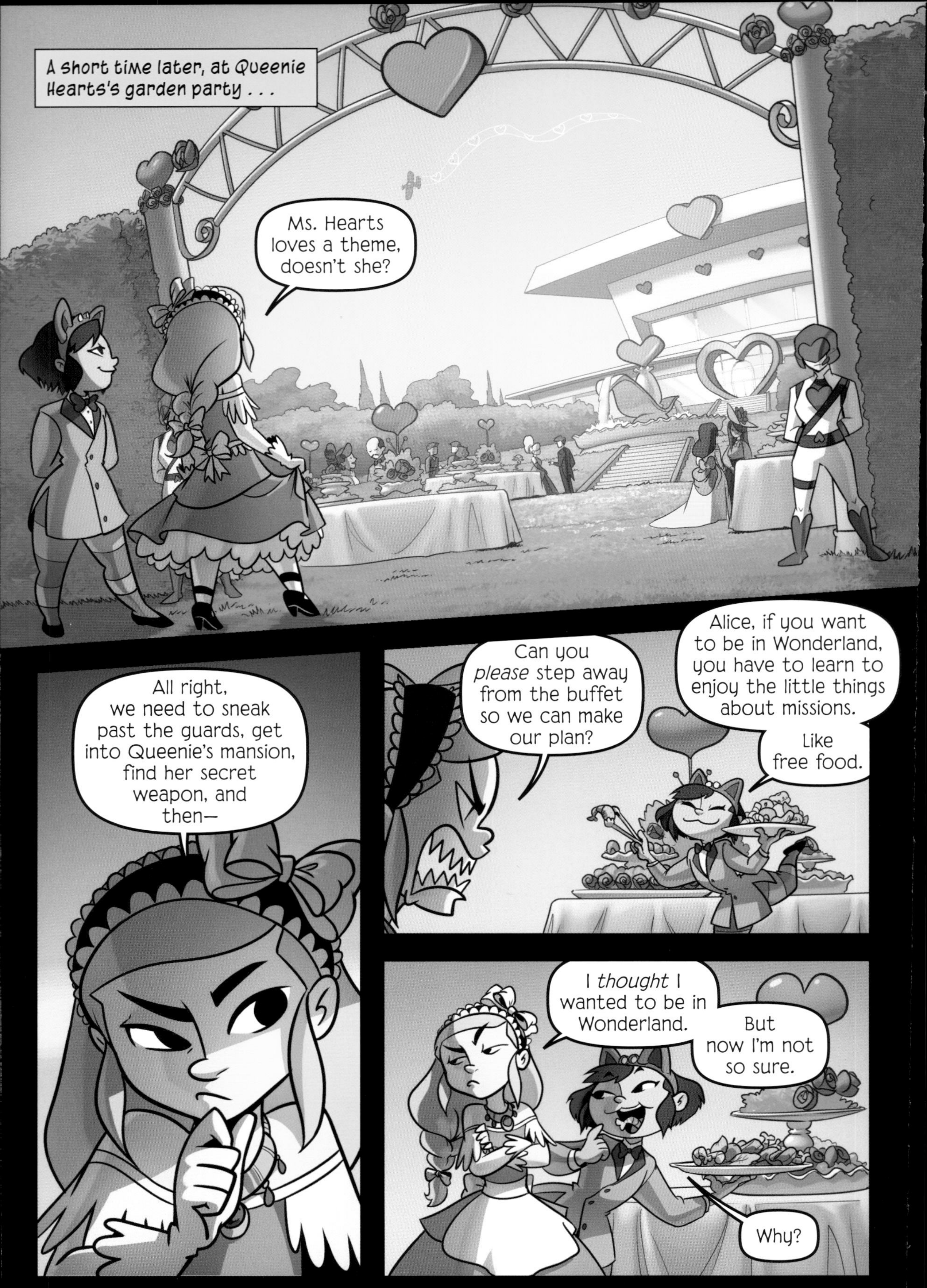
A short time later, at Queenie Hearts's garden party . . .
Ms. Hearts loves a theme, doesn't she?
All right, we need to sneak past the guards, get into Queenie's mansion, find her secret weapon, and then—
Can you *please* step away from the buffet so we can make our plan?
Alice, if you want to be in Wonderland, you have to learn to enjoy the little things about missions.
Like free food.
I *thought* I wanted to be in Wonderland.
But now I'm not so sure.
Why?

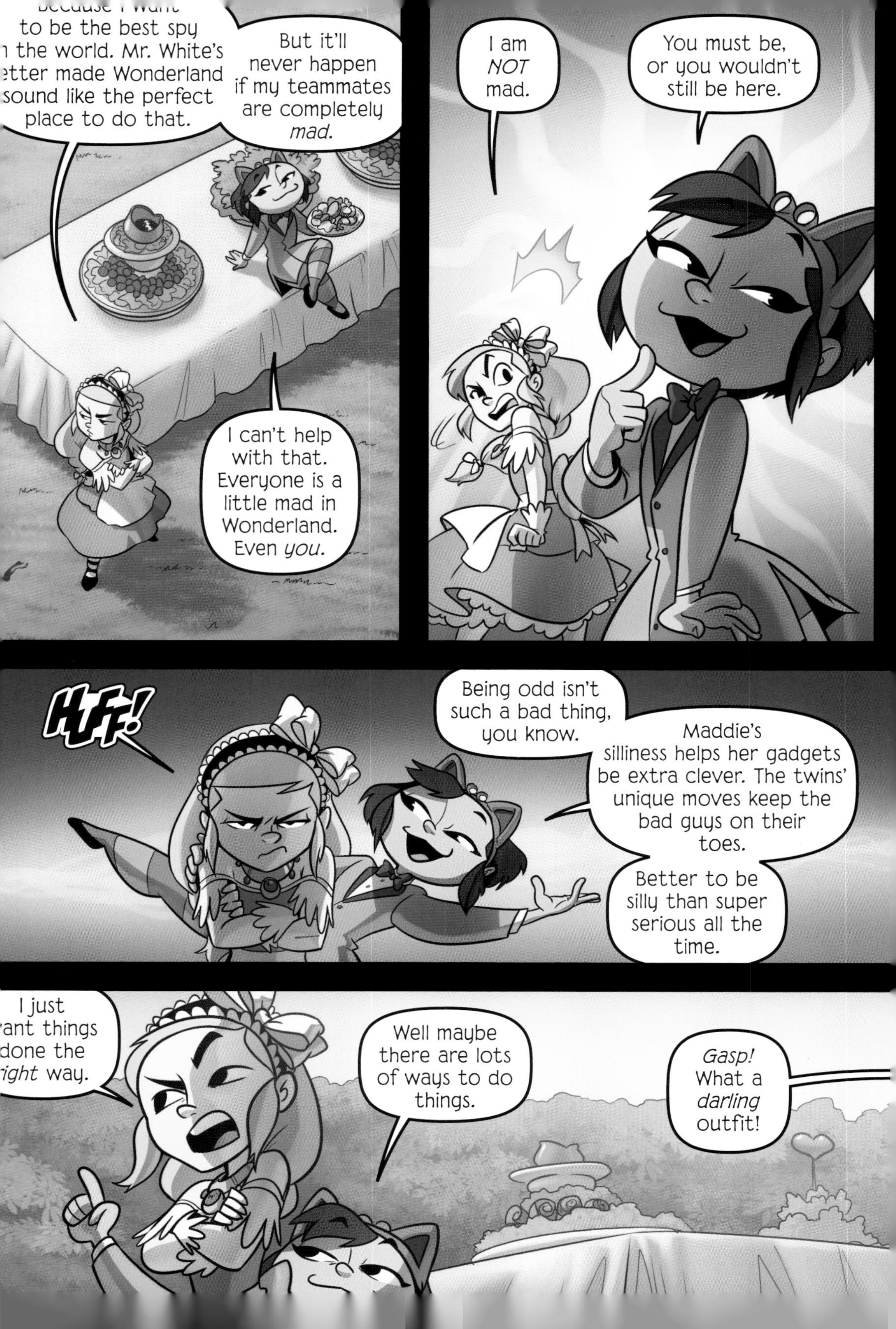
to be the best spy the world. Mr. White's etter made Wonderland sound like the perfect place to do that.
But it'll never happen if my teammates are completely *mad.*
I can't help with that. Everyone is a little mad in Wonderland. Even *you.*
I am *NOT* mad.
You must be, or you wouldn't still be here.
HUFF!
Being odd isn't such a bad thing, you know.
Maddie's silliness helps her gadgets be extra clever. The twins' unique moves keep the bad guys on their toes.
Better to be silly than super serious all the time.
I just ant things done the *ight* way.
Well maybe there are lots of ways to do things.
Gasp! What a *darling* outfit!

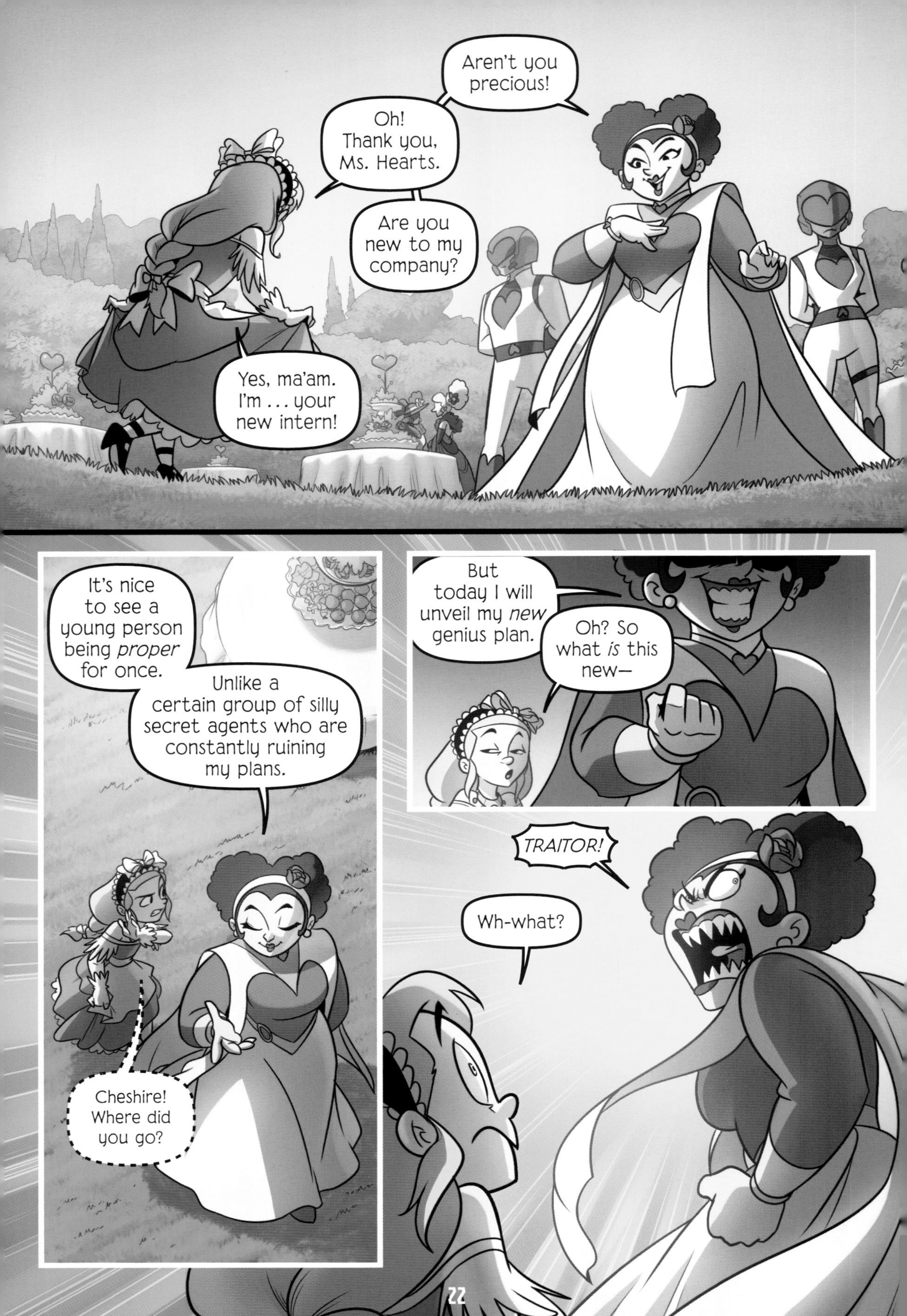
Aren't you precious!
Oh! Thank you, Ms. Hearts.
Are you new to my company?
Yes, ma'am. I'm . . . your new intern!
It's nice to see a young person being *proper* for once.
Unlike a certain group of silly secret agents who are constantly ruining my plans.
Cheshire! Where did you go?
But today I will unveil my *new* genius plan.
Oh? So what *is* this new—
TRAITOR!
Wh-what?

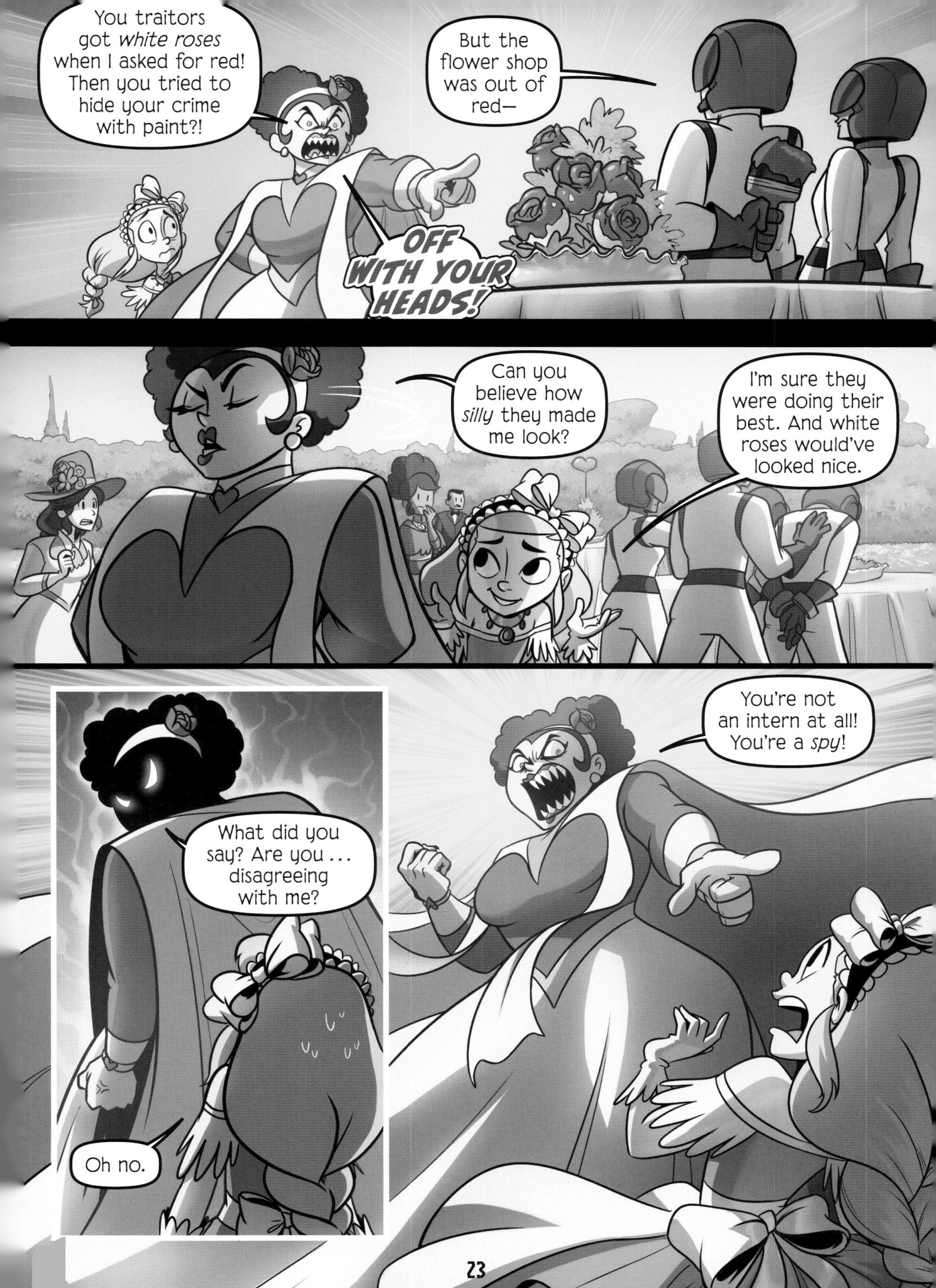
You traitors got *white roses* when I asked for red! Then you tried to hide your crime with paint?!
But the flower shop was out of red—
OFF WITH YOUR HEADS!
Can you believe how *silly* they made me look?
I'm sure they were doing their best. And white roses would've looked nice.
What did you say? Are you . . . disagreeing with me?
Oh no.
You're not an intern at all! You're a *spy*!

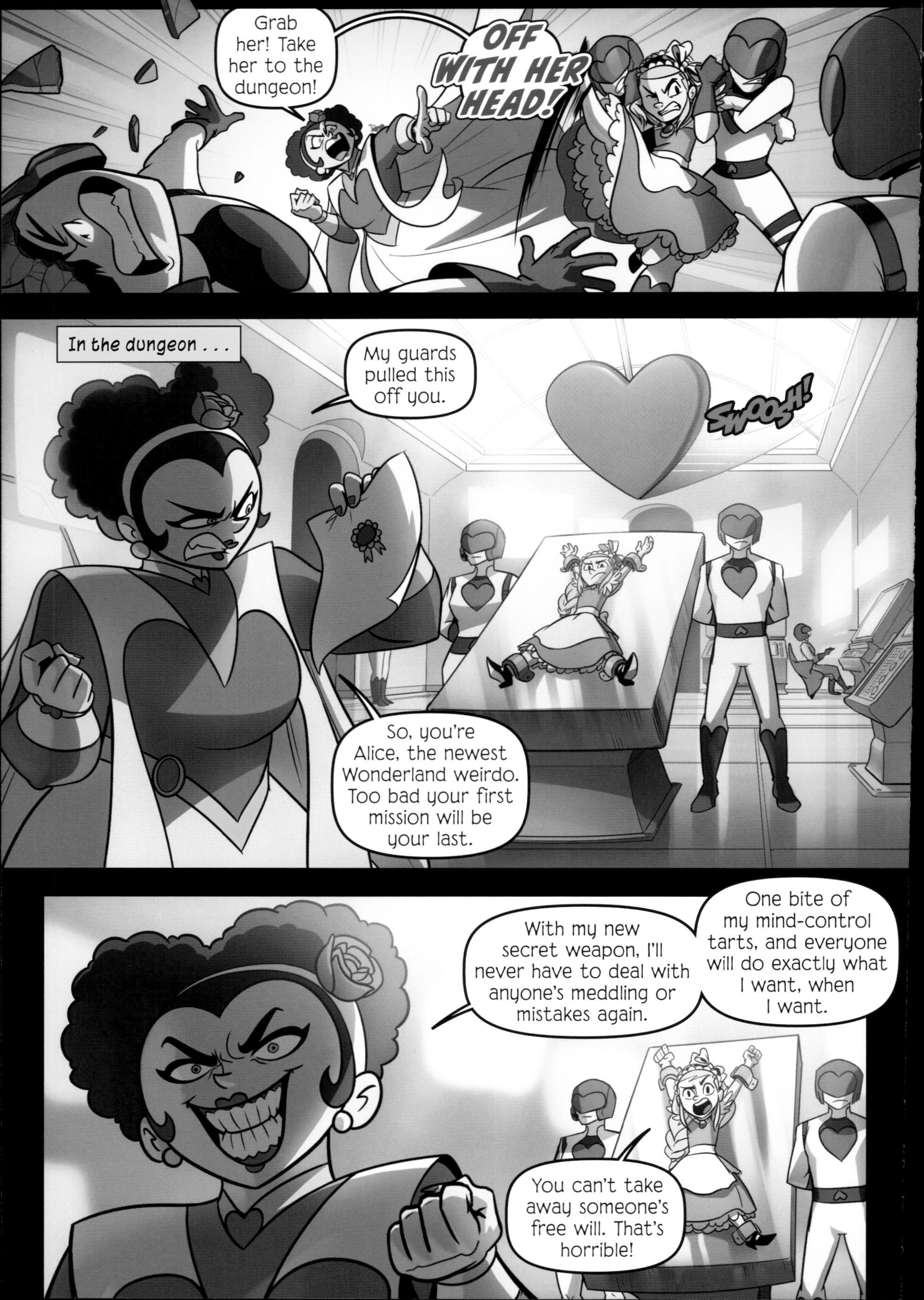

Grab her! Take her to the dungeon!
OFF WITH HER HEAD!
In the dungeon . . .
My guards pulled this off you.
SWOOSH!
So, you're Alice, the newest Wonderland weirdo. Too bad your first mission will be your last.
With my new secret weapon, I'll never have to deal with anyone's meddling or mistakes again.
One bite of my mind-control tarts, and everyone will do exactly what I want, when I want.
You can't take away someone's free will. That's horrible!

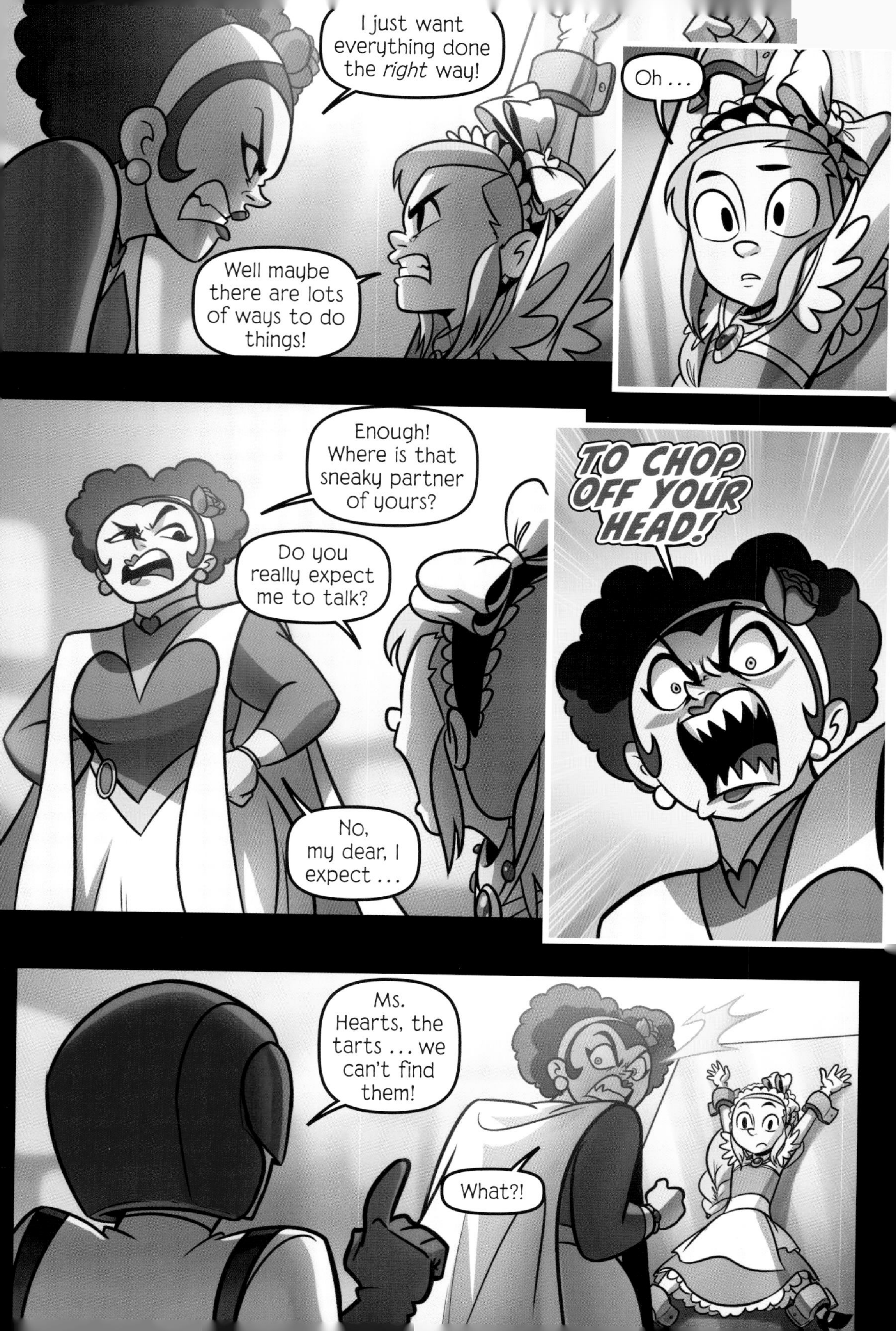
I just want everything done the *right* way!
Well maybe there are lots of ways to do things!
Oh . . .
Enough! Where is that sneaky partner of yours?
Do you really expect me to talk?
No, my dear, I expect . . .
TO CHOP OFF YOUR HEAD!
Ms. Hearts, the tarts . . . we can't find them!
What?!

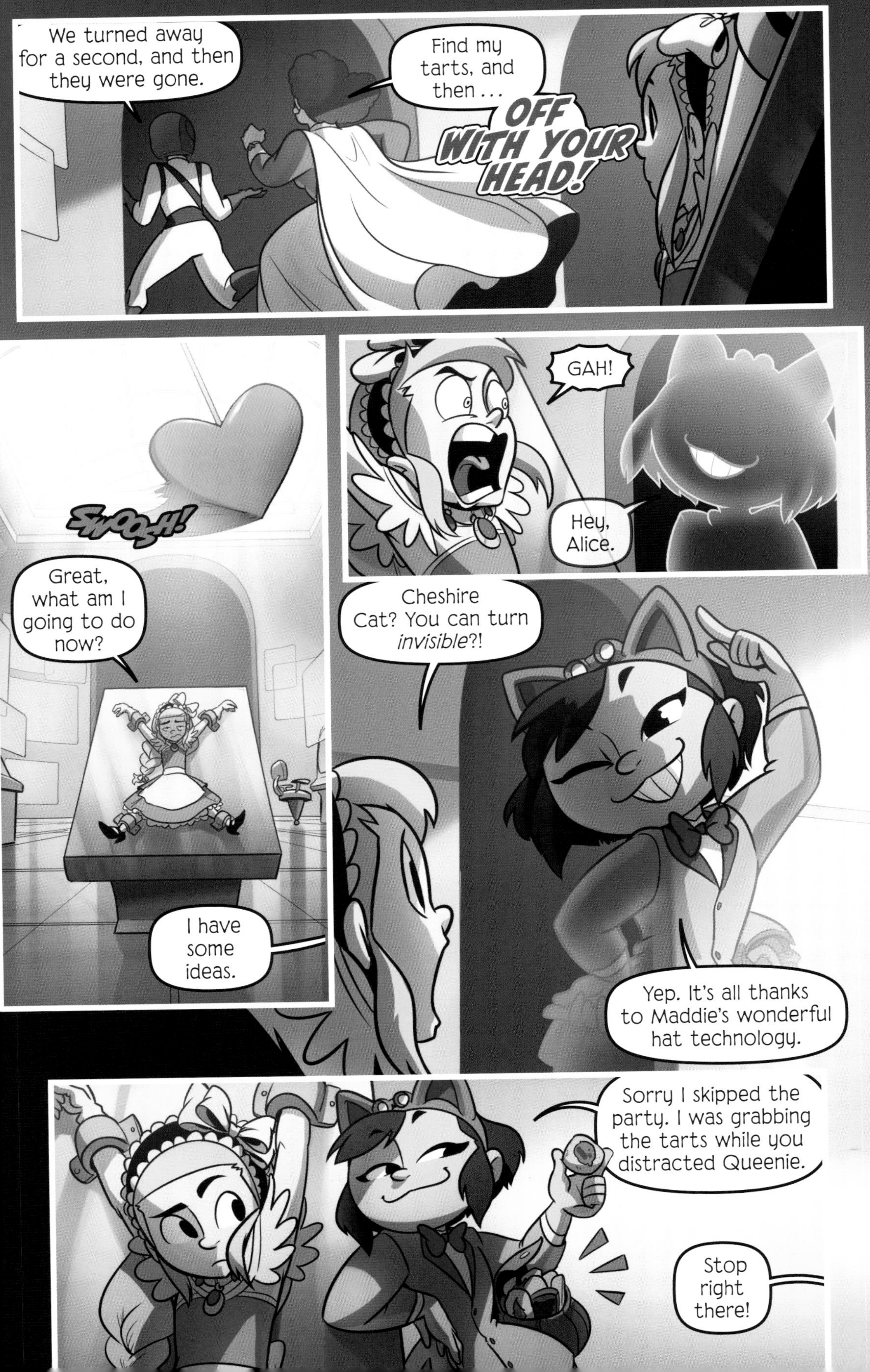
We turned away for a second, and then they were gone.
Find my tarts, and then . . .
OFF WITH YOUR HEAD!
SWOOSH!
Great, what am I going to do now?
GAH!
Hey, Alice.
Cheshire Cat? You can turn *invisible*?!
I have some ideas.
Yep. It's all thanks to Maddie's wonderful hat technology.
Sorry I skipped the party. I was grabbing the tarts while you distracted Queenie.
Stop right there!

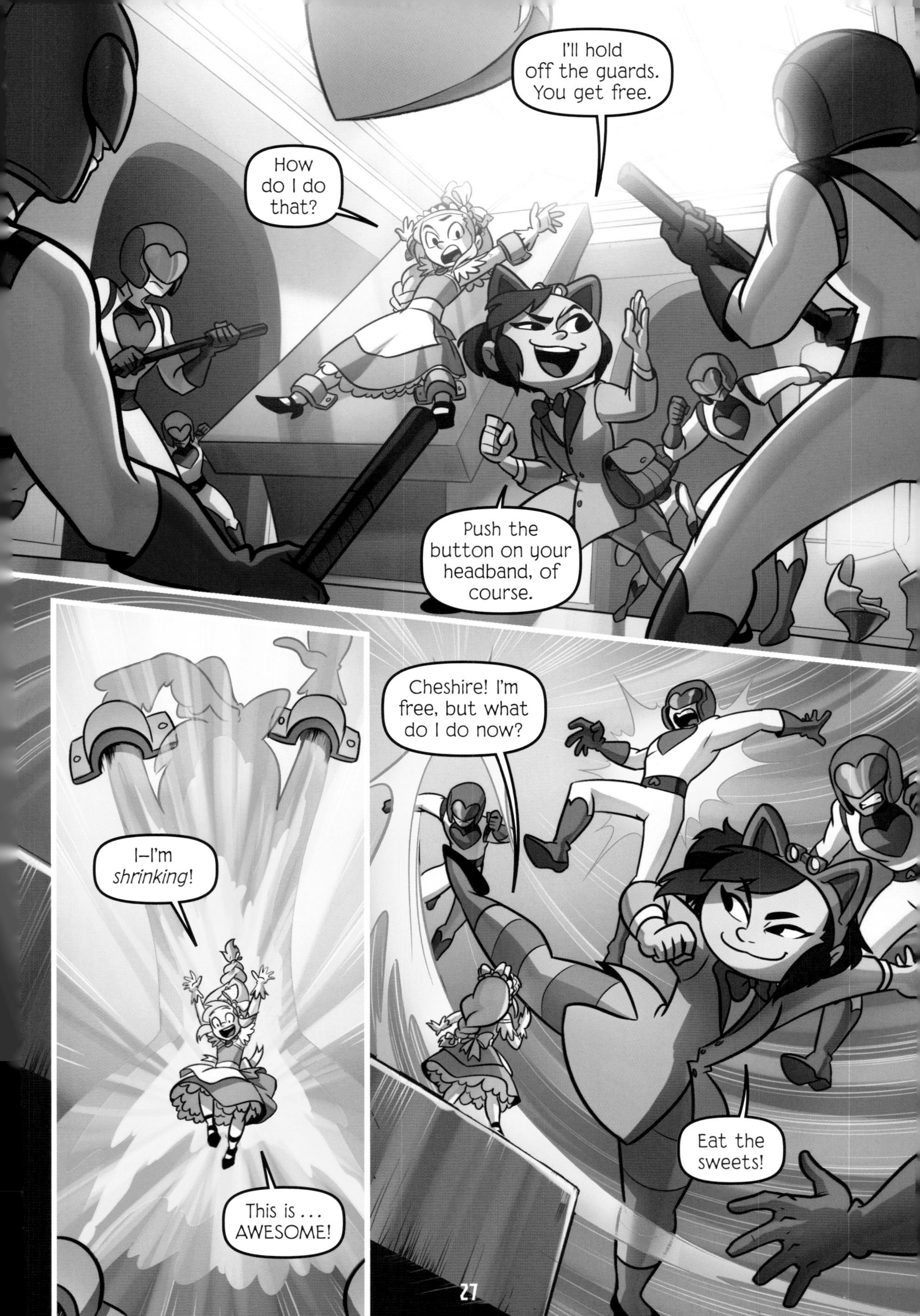
How do I do that?
I'll hold off the guards. You get free.
Push the button on your headband, of course.
I–I'm *shrinking*!
This is . . . AWESOME!
Cheshire! I'm free, but what do I do now?
Eat the sweets!

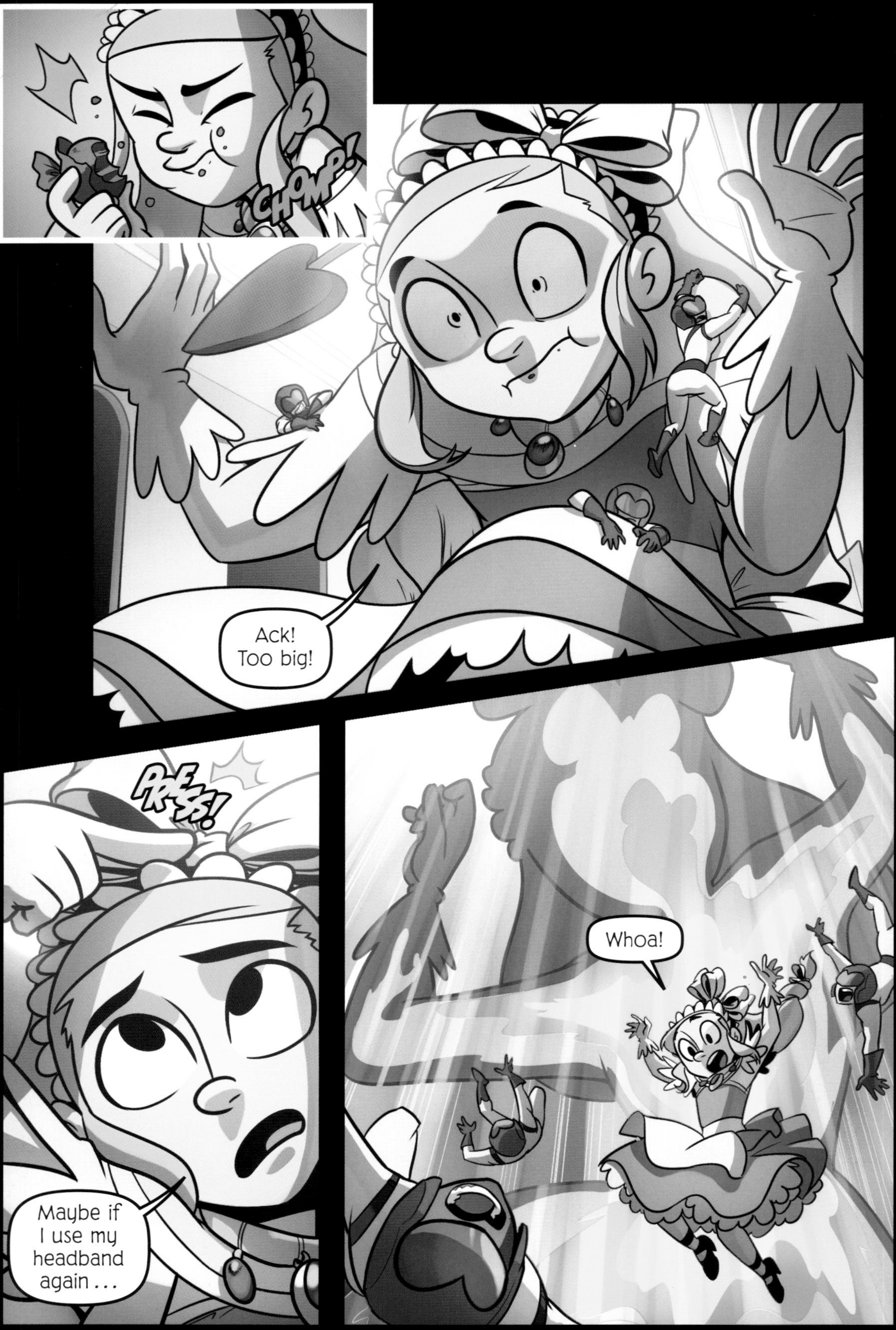
CHOMP!
Ack! Too big!
PRESS!
Maybe if I use my headband again ...
Whoa!

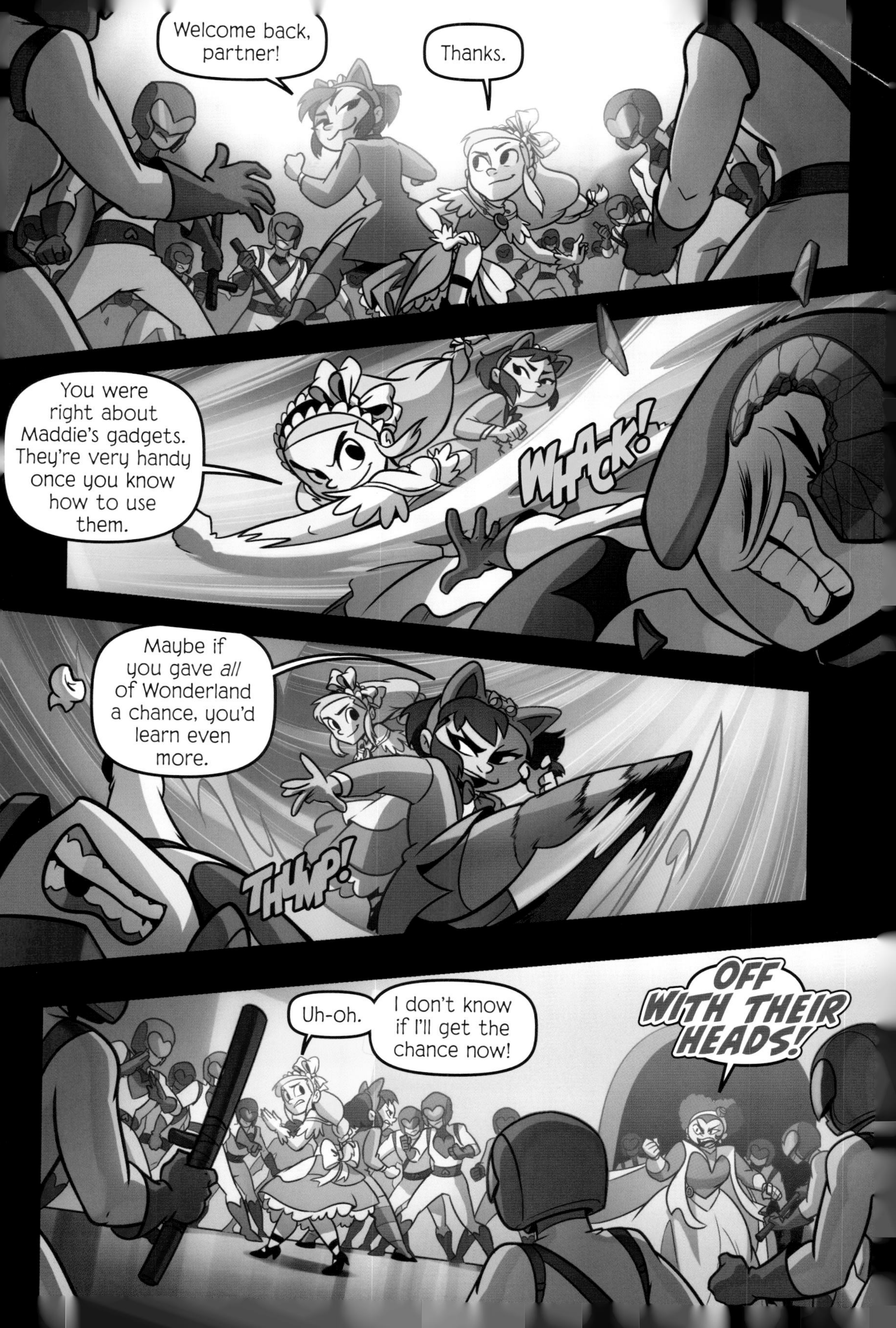
Welcome back, partner!
Thanks.
You were right about Maddie's gadgets. They're very handy once you know how to use them.
WHACK!
Maybe if you gave *all* of Wonderland a chance, you'd learn even more.
THUMP!
Uh-oh.
I don't know if I'll get the chance now!
OFF WITH THEIR HEADS!

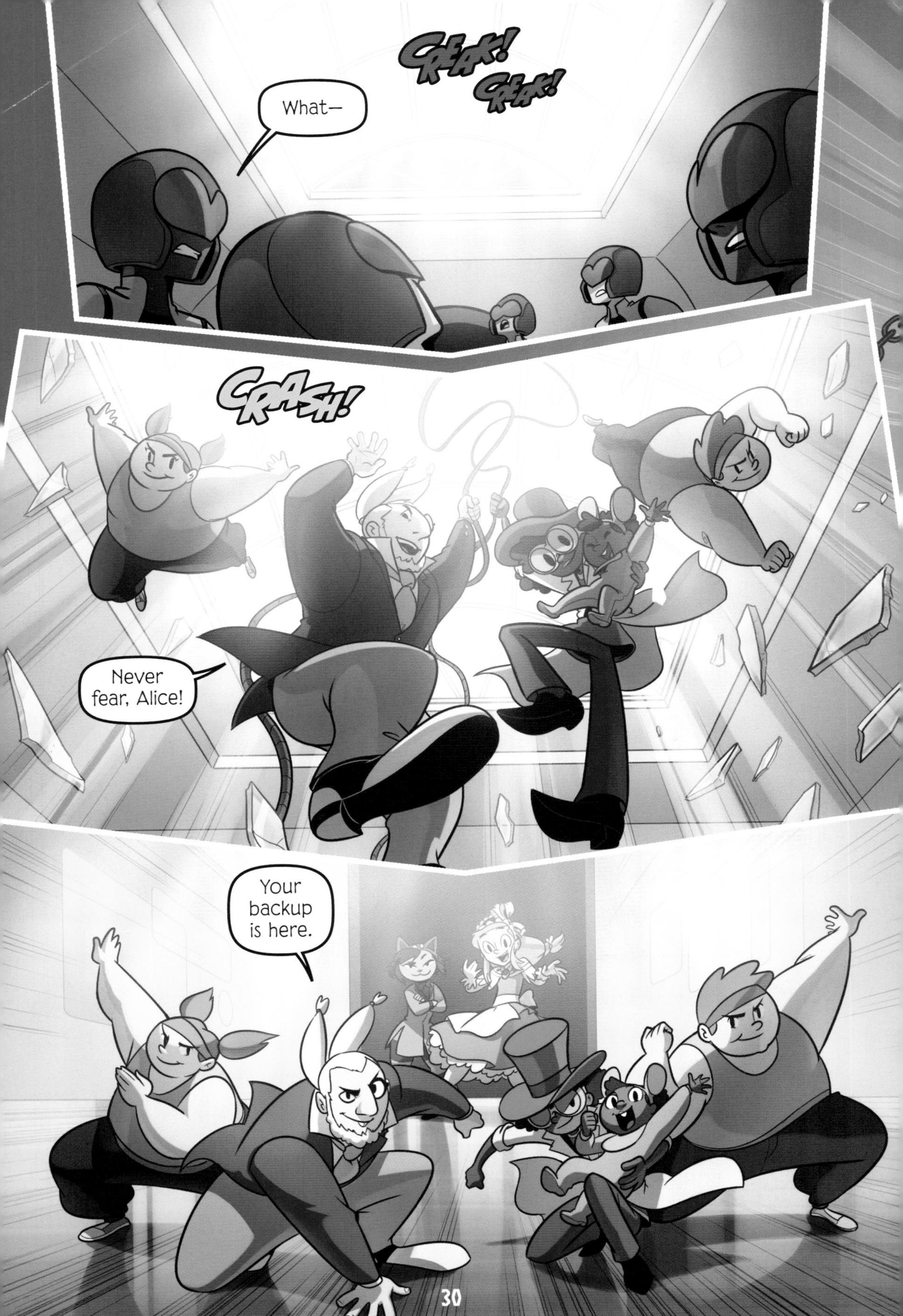
CREAK!
CREAK!
What—
CRASH!
Never fear, Alice!
Your backup is here.

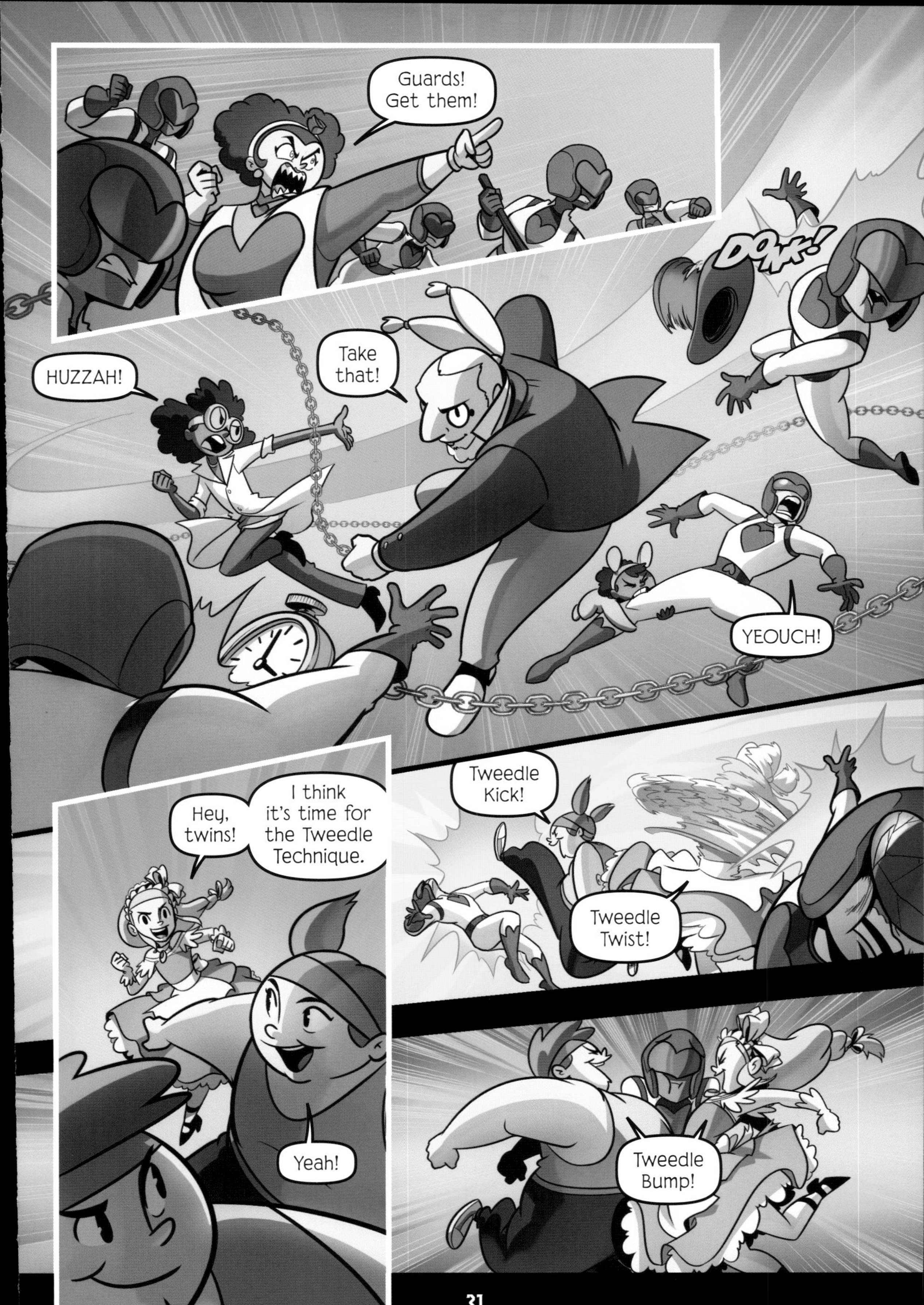
Guards! Get them!
DONK!
HUZZAH!
Take that!
YEOUCH!
Hey, twins!
I think it's time for the Tweedle Technique.
Yeah!
Tweedle Kick!
Tweedle Twist!
Tweedle Bump!

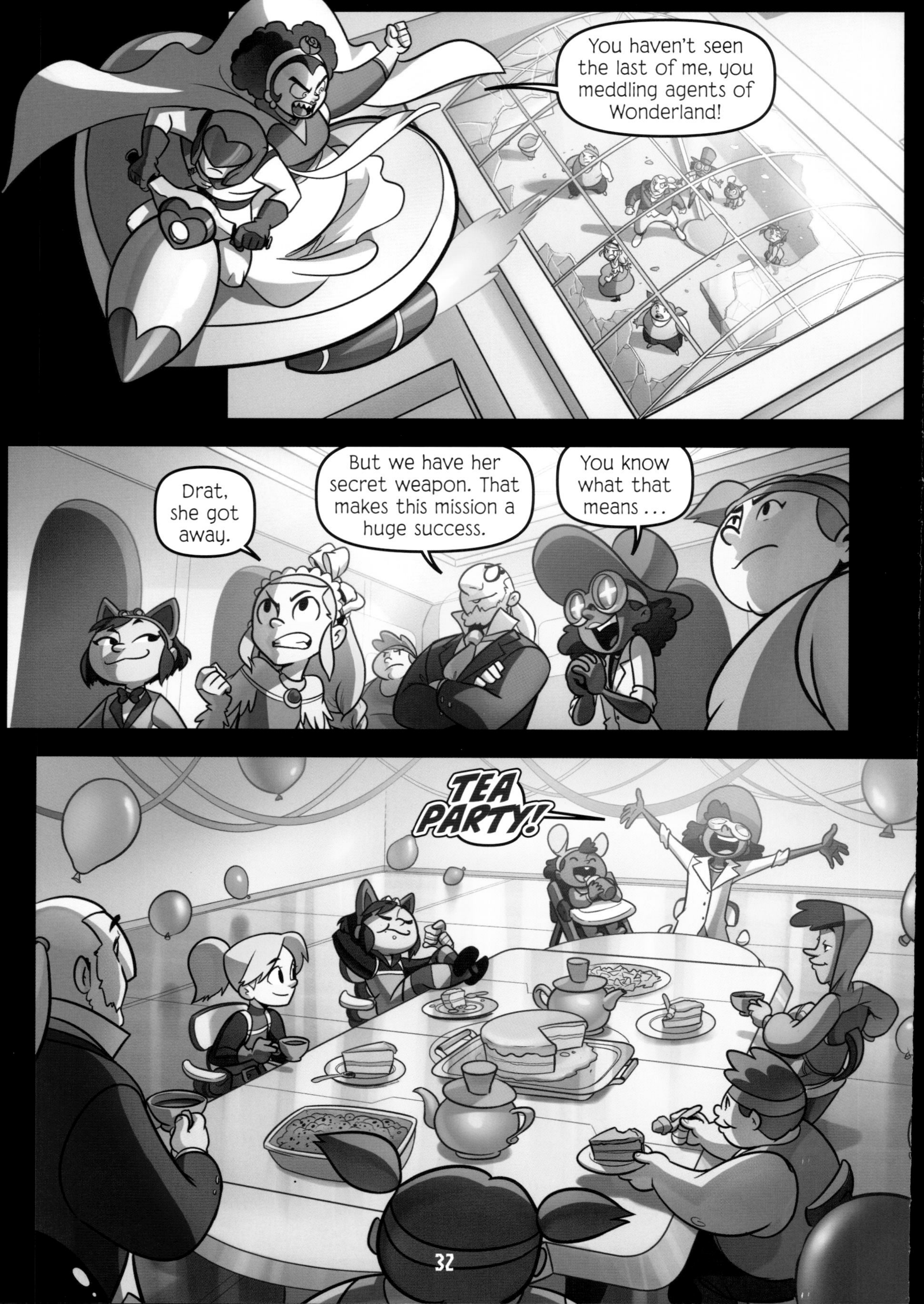
You haven't seen the last of me, you meddling agents of Wonderland!
Drat, she got away.
But we have her secret weapon. That makes this mission a huge success.
You know what that means . . .
TEA PARTY!

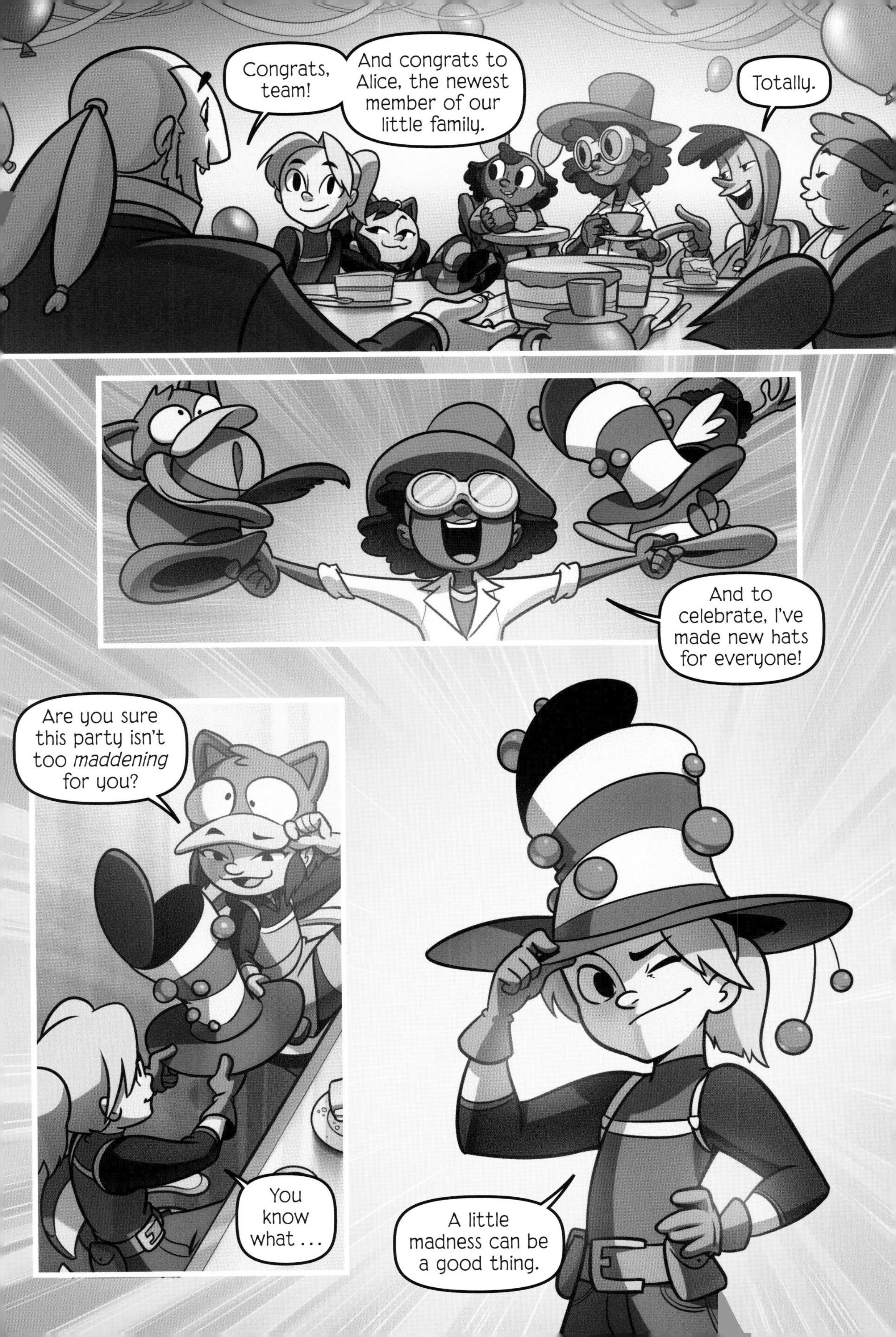
Congrats, team!
And congrats to Alice, the newest member of our little family.
Totally.
And to celebrate, I've made new hats for everyone!
Are you sure this party isn't too *maddening* for you?
You know what . . .
A little madness can be a good thing.

ALL ABOUT THE ORIGINAL STORY!

Alice's Adventures in Wonderland by Lewis Carroll is a novel first published in 1865. The book starts with Alice feeling bored. While reading with her big sister, Alice sees a talking white rabbit saying how he's late to something. Alice follows him down a deep rabbit hole into a strange place called Wonderland.

As Alice looks for the rabbit, she has many odd adventures. First, Alice takes a drink that makes her tiny. Then she eats a cake that makes her giant. She meets a talking caterpillar who is rude and a grinning Cheshire Cat who can disappear. Alice has a tea party with the Mad Hatter and his friends (including a sleepy Dormouse).

Finally, Alice finds the White Rabbit at the Queen of Hearts's garden party. The Queen of Hearts has a bad temper. She shouts, "Off with their heads!" if she doesn't get her way. After someone steals the Queen's tarts, Alice is put on trial and almost loses *her* head! Luckily, that's when Alice wakes up and realizes her time in Wonderland was all a dream.

The book was so successful that Carroll wrote a sequel in 1871 called *Through the Looking-Glass, and What Alice Found There.* Instead of chasing a rabbit, Alice walks through her living room mirror into an opposite world! She meets more strange people, including royal chess pieces, talking flowers, and Tweedledee and Tweedledum. Alice even becomes a queen herself. Once again, the story ends with Alice realizing she'd been asleep the whole time.

The Alice books have been reworked into movies, TV shows, and even video games. Most retellings pull in details from both stories—this comic book does the same thing!

A FAR OUT GUIDE TO THE STORY'S SPY TWISTS

Instead of chasing the White Rabbit down the rabbit hole, Alice is invited by Mr. White to join his secret agents.

The disappearing Cheshire Cat is replaced by Kitty, who uses awesome invisibility tech.

The Mad Hatter and Dormouse are switched out for genius inventor Maddie and her baby sister (and intern), Dora.

The Queen of Hearts is bossy royalty. Queenie Hearts is a rich and evil mastermind—and still bossy!

VISUAL QUESTIONS

In your own words, describe what happens between the first panel and the second. Brainstorm other ways you could draw this moment.

1

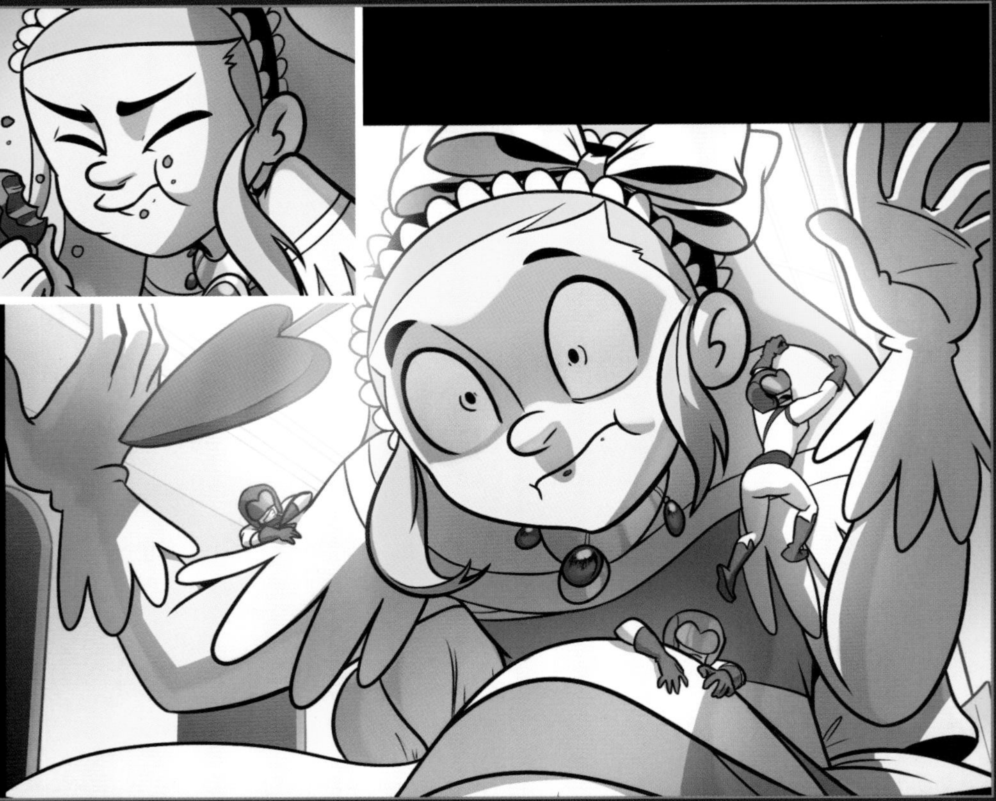

Comics aren't always drawn realistically. The artist exaggerated many of the characters' expressions. What do you think of this choice? How does it affect the story's tone? Find at least two other examples of over-the-top expressions in the book.

2

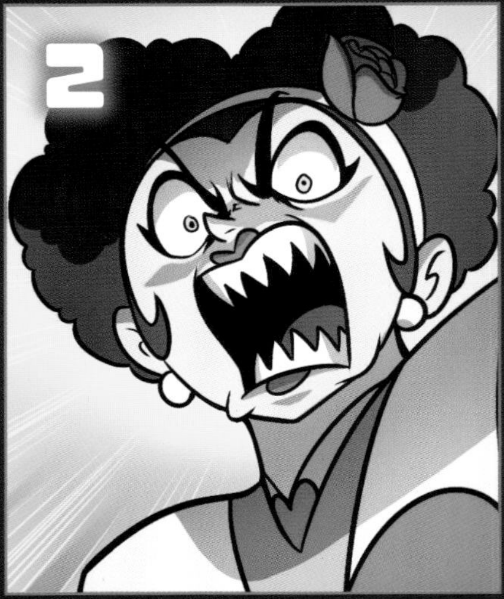

Alice has just realized something. What is it, and why is it important to the story? Try writing a thought bubble that shows what's going through her mind.

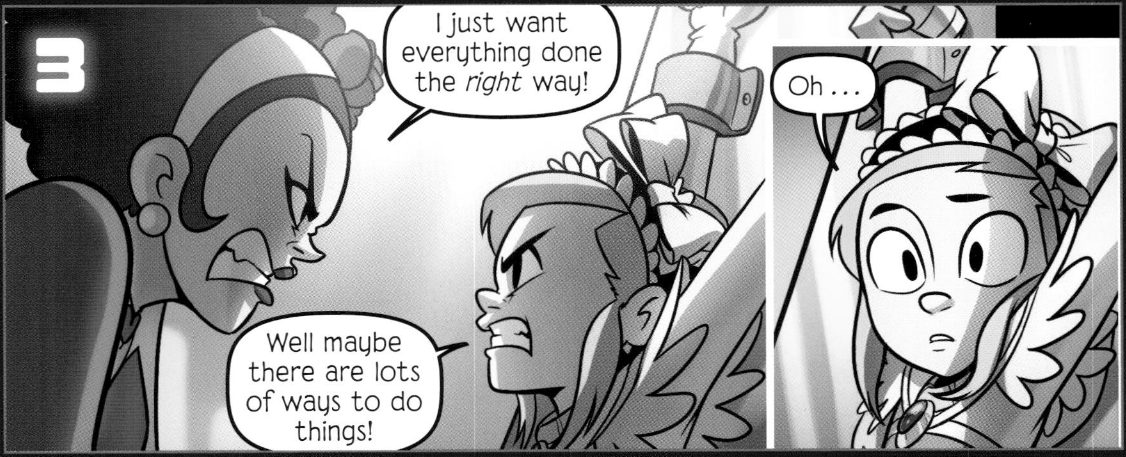
3
I just want everything done the *right* way!
Well maybe there are lots of ways to do things!
Oh . . .

Why are there dotted lines in this panel? How do they connect to the text?

How has Alice changed since she first started at Wonderland? Do you think she'll reach her goal of being a super-skilled secret agent?

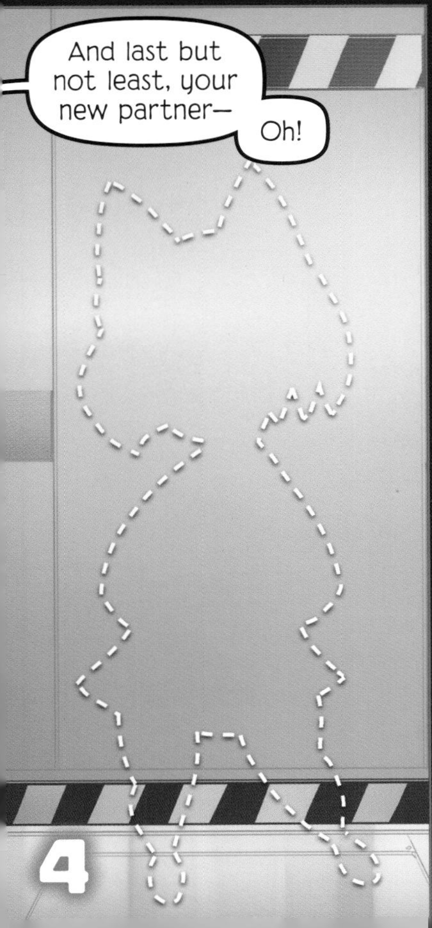
And last but not least, your new partner—
Oh!
4

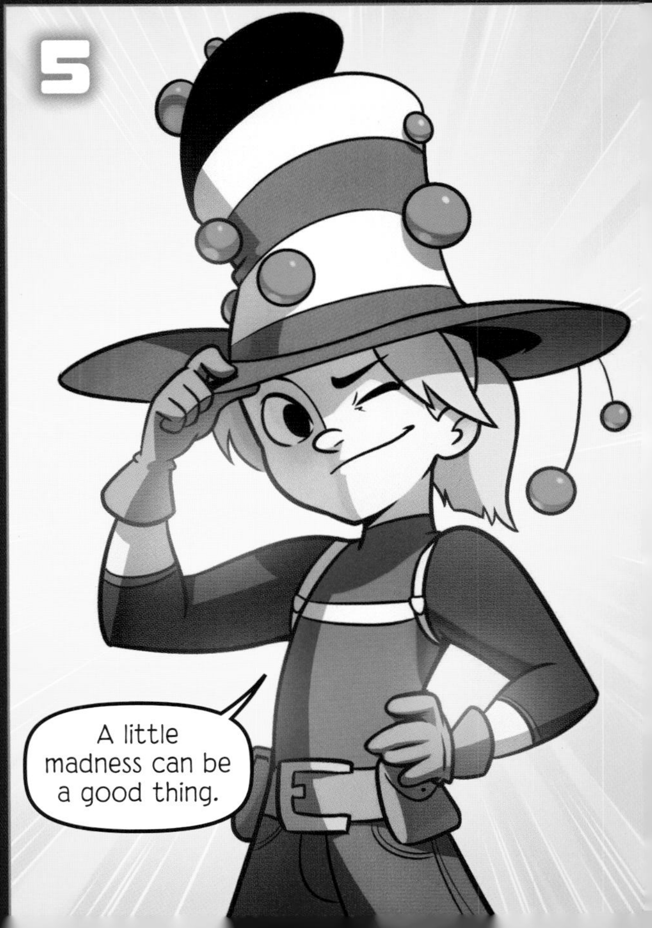
5
A little madness can be a good thing.

AUTHOR

Katie Schenkel is a comic writer best known for the critically acclaimed, Eisner Award-nominated graphic novel *The Cardboard Kingdom*. She especially loves to write about girls' friendships and their perspectives on the world around them. Midwest to her core, Katie lives in Chicago with her partner, Madison.

ILLUSTRATOR

Fern Cano is an illustrator born in Mexico City, Mexico. He currently resides in Monterrey, Mexico, where he makes a living as an illustrator and colorist. He has done work for Marvel, DC Comics, and role-playing games like Pathfinder from Paizo Publishing. In his spare time, he enjoys hanging out with friends, singing, rowing, and drawing!

GLOSSARY

agent (AY-juhnt)—a person who secretly works for a government or other group

code name (KOHD NAYM)—a name that is used in order to keep a person's real name secret

design (di-ZINE)—to plan out and make something for a specific use

expert (EK-spurt)—a person who has a lot of knowledge in something

free will (FREE WIL)—the ability to choose how you act

heiress (AIR-iss)—a woman who has gotten or will get the belongings of someone once they die; usually the belongings are very valuable things such as a large amount of money, ownership of a company, or land

intern (IN-turn)—a person who is working at a job in order to gain experience; usually an intern is a student or has just finished school

invisible (in-VIZ-uh-buhl)—impossible to see

mad (MAD)—thinking and acting in a strange, unusual way

martial arts (MAR-shuhl ARTS)—styles of fighting to protect yourself or to attack

mission (MISH-uhn)—an important job given to a person or group

shrink (SHRINGK)—to become or make smaller

traitor (TRAY-tuhr)—a person who is secretly helping the enemy

OLD FAVORITES. NEW SPINS.

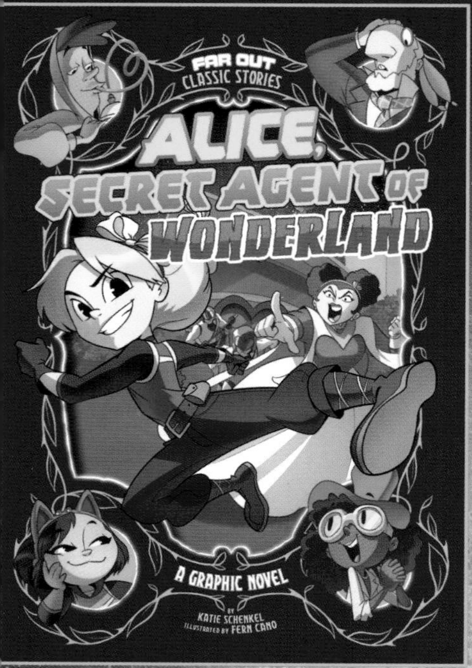
FAR OUT
CLASSIC STORIES
ALICE, SECRET AGENT OF WONDERLAND
A GRAPHIC NOVEL
BY
KATIE SCHENKEL
ILLUSTRATED BY FERN CANO

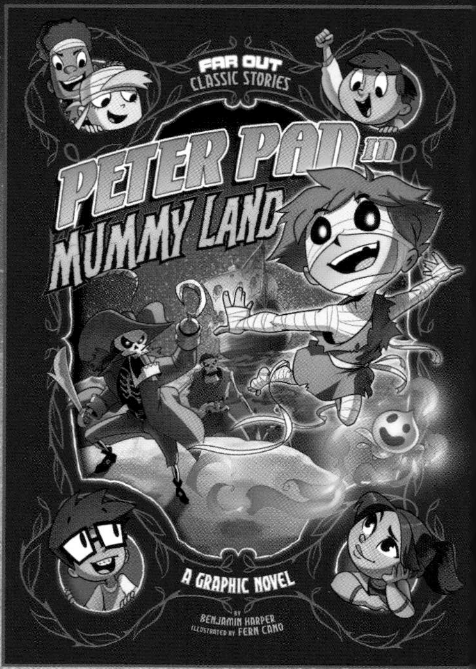
FAR OUT
CLASSIC STORIES
PETER PAN IN MUMMY LAND
A GRAPHIC NOVEL
BY
BENJAMIN HARPER
ILLUSTRATED BY FERN CANO

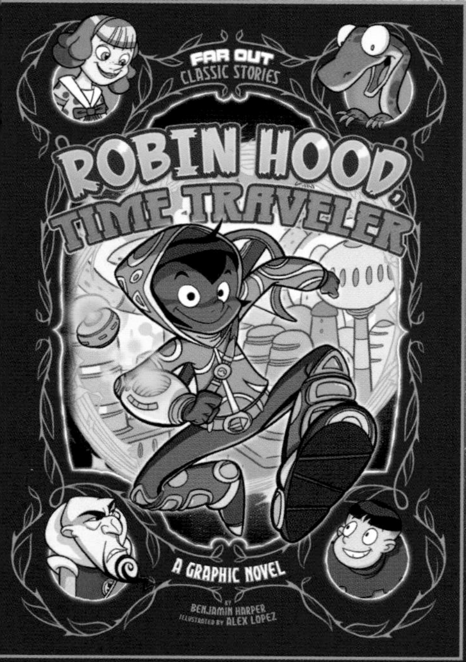
FAR OUT
CLASSIC STORIES
ROBIN HOOD, TIME TRAVELER
A GRAPHIC NOVEL
BY
BENJAMIN HARPER
ILLUSTRATED BY ALEX LOPEZ

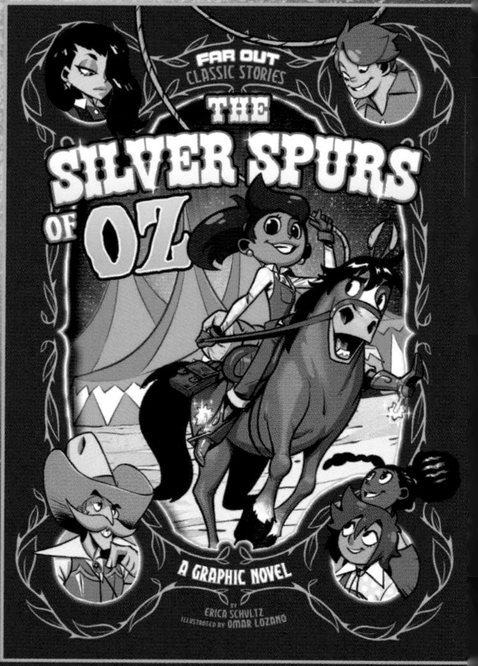
FAR OUT
CLASSIC STORIES
THE SILVER SPURS OF OZ
A GRAPHIC NOVEL
BY
ERICA SCHULTZ
ILLUSTRATED BY OMAR LOZANO

FAR OUT CLASSIC STORIE